Exorcist
THE BEGINNING

EXORCIST

THE BEGINNING

A NOVELIZATION BY STEVEN PIZIKS
SCREENPLAY BY ALEXI HAWLEY
STORY BY WILLIAM WISHER AND CALEB CARR

POCKET STAR BOOKS

New York   London   Toronto   Sydney

An *Original* Publication of POCKET BOOKS

 A Pocket Star Book published by
POCKET BOOKS, a division of Simon & Schuster, Inc.
1230 Avenue of the Americas, New York, NY 10020

ISBN: 0-7434-8270-0

First Pocket Books printing August 2004

10 9 8 7 6 5 4 3 2 1

POCKET STAR BOOKS and colophon are registered
trademarks of Simon & Schuster, Inc.

Interior design by Melissa Isriprashad

Manufactured in the United States of America

For information regarding special discounts for bulk purchases,
please contact Simon & Schuster Special Sales at 1-800-456-6798
or business@simonandschuster.com

Author Acknowledgments

My thanks to John Schippers for access to his extensive occult library. Thanks also to Karen Everson, lay expert on all things Byzantine.

Exorcis†

THE BEGINNING

Prologue

✝

Africa
Anno Domini 507

FATHER THERON MORAKIS squinted at the blue, blue sky and the great golden sun that rained heat down on him. Sweat ran down Theron's face, mixing with the grime to make trickles of mud. The front of his brown habit was stained with more sweat—and with blood. It didn't seem right, that the sun should dare to shine on such a day, in such a place.

A shadow flashed by as a crow flew overhead. Theron trudged over the uneven ground, occasionally stumbling over obstacles he refused to look at. Some of them rolled unpleasantly beneath his feet. The heavy rosary beads and crucifix on his belt banged against his legs, and his toes felt slick inside his boots. It had to be here somewhere. Had to be.

Theron wiped a hand across his forehead, unaware that he left a smear of blood behind. He kept moving forward. Behind him and ahead of him, bodies littered the battlefield. A few twitched or moaned, but most lay still. Dark skin mingled with pale in the piles. Spears and swords stuck out at all angles, and the coppery smell of blood hung heavy on the air. Theron moved among them, his sharp black eyes searching the ground for—

There. A man in a brown robe similar to his own, facedown, impaled by a spear driven through his body and into the ground. The corpse crawled with glittering black flies. Their buzzing made a low, angry roar that pounded Theron's ears like the sun pounded his head. As Theron knelt beside his fallen comrade, a small part of his mind noticed that none of the nearby corpses bore a single fly. Grief knotted Theron's heart and thickened his throat.

"Iason," he whispered, and crossed himself.

Iason didn't respond. The spear stuck out of his back and pointed at the sky like an accusing finger. Theron wanted to remove it but didn't know if he possessed the emotional strength. He waved his hand, trying to clear the flies. They rose for only a moment before settling back down. It looked as if Iason wore a living black cloak. He lay on the blood-soaked ground with one hand outstretched as if he were reaching for something. Theron followed the line of his arm. A blocky stone idol sat just beyond Iason's fingertips. It was squat and square, a winged man with the stylized head of a snarling lion. Its tongue hung out of its mouth in vicious glee. Theron's heart leaped at the sight and he crossed himself again. Had Iason taken it or had he been trying to retrieve it? In any case, Theron had found it.

The idol grinned up at him. Theron wanted to touch

2

it, pick it up like a baby, and hold it close. The grin bore into Theron's head, and a gentle whisper wafted by like a soft breeze. Theron gazed at the idol with both fear and longing. He became aware that he had an erection, hard and throbbing in his loins. The sun continued to pound hard heat down on him.

Still kneeling, Theron reached for the idol. There was a flash of movement, and a hard, pale hand clamped his wrist. Theron let out a yelp of surprise and . . . guilt? He tried to pull free, but the grip was too strong. Iason now raised his head and looked up at Theron with pleading, pain-filled eyes as blue as the perfect sky above them. Theron swallowed.

"Iason," he said. "Everything will be fine. Be at peace."

Iason's mouth moved, but no sound came out. Theron got the impression Iason was trying to warn him about something. He looked around sharply, but there was no one nearby except the corpses. Flies crawled in and out of Iason's mouth. He wasn't trying to speak anymore. It took Theron several moments to realize his friend had died. Theron gently freed his wrist. It seemed as if he should be weeping or performing some sort of service, but he felt no need to do either. His erection still pulsed, long and hard as a spear. Theron looked at the idol again and felt a rush of desire. He picked it up, cradled it against his chest, and got to his feet.

Contentment filled him as he walked toward the hills. He completely ignored the fallen he passed, and didn't hear the harsh calls of the gathering black birds. The roar of Iason's flies died away. Theron walked through hot sunlight until he came to a hollow between two hills. A stone staircase led down into the earth. Beside the staircase stood a low house made of rough wood. Theron looked at the stairs, then at the idol. The idol was beautiful, desirable. It felt so right to hold it in his arms. His groin throbbed anew. He couldn't keep the idol, that he knew. But how could he give up something so wondrous and powerful? The sun caused it pain, wore it away like wind or water. Its true home was under the earth, where it would be hidden and protected. Theron could not keep the idol, true, but neither could he let it come to harm.

He thought a moment, then went inside the rough house that served—had served—as a headquarters for the holy men and their native servants. When he emerged a moment later, he was carrying a rolled sheet of vellum. He carefully made his way down the staircase, idol and vellum in hand. An hour passed. Two. More crows gathered in the battlefield, their sharp beaks seeking the tenderest parts of each corpse.

Theron came back up the staircase with an expression of longing on his face and the vellum in his hand. The idol and his erection had both disappeared. Theron unrolled the thick material and gazed at its contents for a long moment, then rerolled it and trudged wearily away.

Behind him, the sun continued to shine down on the battlefield and the busy crows. They croaked and called to their fellows in harsh voices. One bird flew down from the sky, perched on the sole of a dead soldier's foot, and pecked experimentally at the tough, callused skin. The

4

soldier's dead eyes stared down at the ground, his face twisted in a rictus of agony. The crow pecked again at the soldier's foot, then dropped lower to find something more tender. It landed on the underside of the soldier's jaw, and by reaching down, the crow found it could reach the soft, sweet eyes. The bird clacked its beak in satisfaction and bent its head to feast.

The soldier's wrists and ankles were nailed to a wooden cross, and he was hanging upside down from it. Across the battlefield, hundreds more crosses bore hundreds more dead bodies. They marched motionless across the landscape, an army of twisted dead. The crows circled, dipped, and went to work as the figure of Father Theron Morakis disappeared into the distance.

One

✠

Cairo, Egypt
1949

A goat that is loose does not listen to the voice of the shepherd.

—Kenyan proverb

THE BOY SIDLED through the door and took in the bar with a practiced, mercenary glance. Hard lines of light leaking in through the cracks of the straw window shades and snaking across the dusty floor. A scattering of cheap tables and rickety chairs, most of them empty at this time of day. The few customers staring into half-empty glasses. Flies hovering on still, hot air.

The boy's gaze passed over a young woman who nursed an infant in the corner and came to rest on a white man. The man's head was down, and his hat covered most of his face. The boy smiled and readjusted the battered bag flung over his shoulder. Inside it, wooden joints clattered like broken teeth. As the boy headed across the bar, he noticed half a dozen empty glasses on the white man's table next to a haphazard pile of coins. The boy's footsteps suddenly grew quieter and he handled the bag more carefully so it wouldn't rattle. Silver gleamed in the dusty light. The boy reached the table and edged a hand out.

The white man slapped his own hand hard over the coins. He didn't bring his head up. The boy's only reaction was to smile with crooked teeth and raise his bag. It rattled woodenly again.

"Puppet, sir?" he asked, his English accented but clear enough. "Only ten *piastres*."

At this Lankester Merrin raised his head. He wore two days' growth of beard and a wrinkled khaki shirt with food stains dribbled down the front. His blue eyes were dull with drink, though his square face was impassive.

"Do I look like I play with puppets, son?" he replied.

Undaunted, the boy fished an articulated wooden figurine out of the bag and laid it with a clatter on the table. It was about a foot high, man-shaped, with the head of a jackal. The maker had painted it in crude, bright colors.

"Anubis?" Merrin asked. "Why would I want to buy a marionette done up as a death god?"

"I give you one for five *piastres*, then," the boy said. "It's handmade. Please. My sister—she's very sick."

"Your sister," Merrin said nastily, "is peddling in the next bar over." He grabbed one of the glasses in front of him, raised it, and saw it was empty. The boy hadn't

8

and dredged up a response. "That's not possible. The Byzantine empire adopted Christianity, but it never got that far south."

"Nevertheless," Semelier returned, "there it sits." He rested both hands on the top of his cane. "The British have financed a dig to uncover this church. We believe a rare object waits inside, a relic the British are happily unaware of. We want you to find it and bring it back to us."

Merrin roused himself at this. "You think I'm a thief?"

Semelier's response was to slide a thick brown envelope across the tabletop. "For your trouble."

"So now I'm a thief *and* a whore."

"No. Simply a man who's lost faith in everything but himself. An interesting position, if you ask me."

"I didn't ask." Merrin slugged down more scotch. It was definitely time to bypass mellow and head straight for dead drunk. "You know nothing about me."

"Actually, I do," Semelier said. "An Oxford-educated archaeologist and expert in religious icons. You had a promising career in archaeology, but you chose the Church just before the War. The Church sent you on several digs, most notably ones that had the potential to uncover something of religious significance. Several of your discoveries are on display at the Vatican, and at least one vanished into the Pope's personal archives without further acknowledgment. You have demonstrated your dedication to both science and the priesthood." Semelier leaned forward on his cane. "Only . . . where is that collar now?"

Merrin discovered he was on his feet with no memory of actually standing up. His chair rocked back and forth on the floor behind him. "You can—"

A rolled leather case hit the table with a thump. The case was cracked and worn—clearly old. Merrin guessed seventh or eighth century, though that was positively modern compared to most of the materials he had examined over the years. He looked at Semelier, then back down at the case. That it contained a clue to the artifact Semelier was interested in, Merrin had no doubt. And he couldn't deny that he wanted to see it.

Merrin remembered rooting through the attic at his grandparents' farmhouse in Cambridgeshire—it was the same summer his dog had died—and uncovering a packet of papers that turned out to be a journal his great-great-grandmother had started just before she got married. The faint, spidery handwriting offered him a glimpse of true history and awakened a hunger that he had never completely sated. He had also been shocked to read about his ancestor's colorful and specific comments on her new husband's considerable prowess in bed. His shock hadn't prevented him from reading the journals over and over, though. These passages had awakened other hungers, ones which he had also never sated.

The priesthood had helped him feed the first and deny the second, though, come to think of it, he hadn't felt much hunger for anything lately. Until now. Looking at that rolled case brought the old feelings back, the delicious sense of uncovering something no eye had seen for hundreds of years, of having a direct window into the minds of people who had lived and thought and breathed in centuries now dead.

Ignoring Semelier's smug expression, Merrin slowly picked up the case, opened it, and gingerly extracted a piece of vellum. It was brown with age and cracking around the edges. Merrin pushed the empty scotch glasses aside and unrolled the vellum flat on the table with careful, practiced fingers. Smells of dust and ancient leather rose into the air.

The baby in the corner wailed. Its cry was like a physical slap in the otherwise quiet bar. The baby's mother, who looked barely sixteen, tried to comfort the infant, but it continued to cry. Merrin looked down at the vellum. A dark smear of charcoal or a similar substance glared back up at him. It was a rubbing of a square carving or idol with a flat front. The body shape was human, but it had wings on its back and clawed talons on its feet. A fierce, stylized lion's head, complete with fangs and protruding tongue, snarled up at Merrin, and he found himself oddly reluctant to put a finger anywhere near the creature's mouth.

"Sumerian," he said.

"The rubbing was done around the sixth century, yes," Semelier agreed, "but the original piece is much older."

A fly crawled across the rubbing. It was joined by a second and a third. The baby continued to cry, despite its mother's attempts to hush it. Merrin waved his hand to shoo the flies away and wished the baby would shut up. A fourth fly landed when the first three took off. Merrin licked his lips, suddenly wishing the alcohol would stop fuzzing his thought processes. How had a Byzantine church come to exist in East Africa? Who had built it? And why would a Sumerian idol be associated with it? It was a mystery, a puzzle, and Merrin was a man who lived—had lived—for puzzles.

The first step was to find all the pieces. So far he had three: the vellum, the rubbing, and Semelier's word that the church existed. He had no reason to doubt Semelier, unless there was some strange plot afoot he wasn't aware of. But Merrin was nobody, an unimportant expatriate drunk living in the armpit of nowhere. The idea that anyone would want to lure *him* into some strange international conspiracy was ludicrous. The artifact displayed in the rubbing might prove to have great archaeological value, but it was unlikely to be worth much on the antiquities black market. Yet here was Semelier, waving money and an irresistible puzzle under Merrin's nose to get him involved.

He switched his gaze from the rubbing to Semelier's face. The older man was still seated. "Why do you think this object is inside a Byzantine church in Africa?"

"Major Dennis Granville in Nairobi is in charge of the dig," Semelier answered with an enigmatic smile. "He's been . . . persuaded to let you join. And he expects your arrival within the month."

"You're assuming I'll say yes," barked Merrin, aware that only the scotch was preventing him from getting pissed off.

"You already have," Semelier said.

Semelier's words reached through the alcohol and touched Merrin's temper. His face hardened, and he folded his arms in stubborn refusal. He wasn't going to let this little pissant dictate his life. The Church had done that often enough. Semelier's eyes flickered uncertainly when he caught Merrin's expression. The baby finally stopped crying.

"Just who the hell do you think you are, anyway?" Merrin snapped.

"Your benefactor." He thumped his cane once on the floor as if to bring the conversation back under control. "You know how to use the trains here in Egypt, I assume?"

Merrin nodded. "I do, but I'm not—"

"Good. At dawn tomorrow, you will take the train to Suez. At the port, you will find a ship named the *Slow Dreamer*. The captain has instructions to take you on board. The *Dreamer* will take you to Djibouti."

"I said I'm not—"

"Just south of the city is a small airfield. There you will find an airplane and a pilot waiting for you. He will fly you to Nairobi, where you will meet with Major Granville, who is most eager to meet you. He will direct you to the dig."

"I'm not going to—" Merrin began, then stopped as the implications of Semelier's words sank in. "Wait a minute. You've been calling it a dig. Are you saying the church is—"

"—buried?" Semelier finished. "Yes. Didn't I mention that? Though I imagine a fair amount of it has been uncovered by now. Major Granville has requisitioned a great many shovels and pickaxes."

"Shovels?" Merrin's eyes went wide. "*Pickaxes?* Dear

God, he might as well use a steam shovel! What about sieves and brushes? Has he requisitioned them, at least?"

"I don't believe he has."

"Christ! Who's overseeing the excavation at the moment?"

"I am not sure. The head archaeologist has . . . left the project, you see, and the native workers have been instructed to continue digging in his absence. They're quite efficient, though at the moment they have no archaeologist to direct them. Only a foreman and a site manager."

Merrin's blood ran alternately cold and hot. Heavy tools were used only sparingly in such work, and the thought of a bunch of untrained natives swinging pick-axes around potentially valuable artifacts . . .

The scotch oozed around in his stomach, and he felt nauseated. No matter how he might feel about Semelier, priceless knowledge was possibly being destroyed at this very moment. Swiftly he rolled up the vellum and slid it back into its case. "What was the name of that ship in Suez?"

Semelier repeated the instructions while Merrin gathered up the case and the envelope. His eye fell on the puppet, still lying on the table in a stiff tangle of arms and legs. A fly crawled around the thing's mouth. Merrin shoved it across the table to Semelier, then turned and wordlessly walked away. When he reached the door, he turned back. "Who exactly do you represent, Mr. . . ." His voice trailed off.

Semelier was gone.

Two

✝

Nairobi, British East Africa

Two guests cannot be entertained satisfactorily at the same time.

—Kenyan proverb

FATHER WILLIAM FRANCIS snapped the curtain aside and found a camel. It was staring placidly through the window and chewing something that made it slobber green-brown goo. The priest jumped back with a startled gasp. The camel made a rude noise and poked its nose through the lower half of the window into the room. Saliva plopped onto the dark wooden floor.

Behind Father Francis, Major Dennis Granville roared with laughter. "I think he's looking for a baptism, Father."

"I think he's offering to baptize *me*," Will said, and backed away. Not knowing what else to do, he added, "Shoo!"

Granville laughed again. "You'll have to do better than that, Father."

Will glared at the camel. The camel gave him a look that dared him to come closer. Will remained stubbornly out of reach. Camels, he knew all too well, were as unpredictable as they were smelly. They bit, spat, kicked, and trod on your feet. And that was when they were in a *good* mood.

From just outside the window came a shout and the solid *thwack* of a stout stick striking heavy fur. The camel shot Will a reproachful look, pulled out of the window, and strolled unhurriedly away. A young man with dark skin and eyes pursued it, yelling over his shoulder, "I am sorry, Father!"

Only in Africa.

Shaking his head, Will approached the window again and, avoiding the little puddle of camel saliva, peered outside. A white stone path connected the front yard with the red earth street. A line of camels paraded with awkward solemnity past, joined most recently by their stray compatriot. Beyond them stretched a hilly green plain dotted with scrubby trees. Two flagpoles in front of the house sported banners that flapped lazily in the warm breeze—the British flag and the British coat of arms. The latter indicated this was a government building. A small convoy of British military vehicles passed the camels. Beasts and lorries each ignored the other. The priest sighed; unfortunately, the same thing couldn't always be said about the English and their African colonial subjects.

Coming up the street in the opposite direction was a

18

man dressed in dusty brown field kit and carrying a round leather case. He had brown hair, a broad build, and a tight, unhappy posture. Handsome enough, though that wasn't supposed to matter. Will, however, had enough experience as a priest to know that good looks opened more doors. God might look at your heart, he mused wryly, but people looked at your face.

"Here he comes," Will said.

Granville stopped chuckling and approached the window for a look. "Looks ordinary enough."

"He's not," Will replied, offended. "He has one of the finest archaeological minds, or did. Before the War." Everyone always said it that way—"the War," pronounced with the capital W made clear. "The War wasn't kind to him."

"It wasn't kind to any of us, Father," the major said dismissively. "We scar over and carry on."

"With God's help," Will added.

Granville snorted, then paced back to the wall, on which hung a local map of Kenya. Overhead, a ceiling fan lazily stirred the humid air. Granville's office was paneled in dark wood, with pale woven mats on the floor. A series of glass-fronted cases displayed dozens of butterflies, all neatly pinned and labeled, their colorful wings spread like dead rainbows on white mounting boards. On the floor sat a cage made of mosquito netting stretched over a wooden frame. The bottom of the cage was covered with grass, leaves, and flowers. Several live butterflies clung to the mesh, their colorful wings opening and closing with slow patience.

Granville reached behind his desk and came up with what looked like a large briefcase. With a grunt he set it on a stand and opened it. Buckled inside with leather straps were traveling flasks of gin, vermouth, scotch, and whiskey. Metal and glass clinked. Still at the window, Will watched Lankester Merrin wander down the white path and take a careful seat on the front steps of the government building. He opened the leather case, unrolled some sort of scroll, and studied it. Will found himself saying a small prayer for him.

Once Granville finished pouring his drink, he set it aside and opened a drawer. From it he took a glass jar, a paper bag of cotton balls, and a bottle marked *Ether*. He turned to the butterfly cage, opened it, and used a tiny mesh net to scoop out one of the larger insects. It had bright blue wings.

"Corporal!" he boomed. "Send in Lankester Merrin!"

Merrin sat on the front steps of the government building. He started to pray that the wait wouldn't be long, then stopped himself. The wait would be however long it was, and his prayers would make no difference.

Merrin hated waiting, hated inactivity, and the trip south from Cairo had been a weeklong exercise in both. It hadn't helped that a Muslim had captained the *Dreamer*, meaning no alcohol was allowed on the ship. No drink to fog Merrin's mind and no work to occupy it. It was during those times that the dreams came. Merrin hadn't had a decent night's sleep since he'd left Cairo.

Now he was here in Nairobi, bone tired, covered

with road dust, and staring down at Semelier's rubbing. The lion's eyes stared back at him with sly, malicious glee. A fly crawled across its face, and abruptly Merrin couldn't stand to look at it anymore. It belonged in a museum, in any case. He rerolled it and thrust it back into the case.

Impatience pulled at him. If Major Granville was so eager to have Merrin on this dig, why was the man keeping him waiting? Merrin drummed his fingers on his knees and tapped his feet in a restless rhythm. His heavy boots made a marching sound on the white path that led up to government building steps, and abruptly Merrin was surrounded by the sound of jackboots stomping across cobblestones. He stopped tapping.

A company of British troops marched past him up the road leading into town. Their sergeant major yelled orders above the sounds of their steady footsteps. Sweat darkened their brown uniforms and glistened on their faces beneath the heavy golden sun.

"Look lively, you mangy lot!" shouted the sergeant major. "Double time now! Left, right, left, right!"

The soldiers sped up. One soldier, caught off guard by the order, faltered and threw the man behind him out of step. Both stumbled, then recovered.

"What the hell do you think you're doing, Private?" screamed the sergeant without breaking stride. *"Hast du denn Urlaub? Einen Feiertag? Gehen wir in der Stadt vielleicht einkaufen?"*

A hot wind blew up the street and dust motes pelted Merrin's face and neck. Except that it felt like cold, misty rain. The sergeant continued to yell in German as the soldiers' black boots marched steadily down the stony street between tall, narrow houses. Merrin rocked back and forth on the steps, caught between memory and reality.

A hand came down on his shoulder. Merrin started violently and twisted like a cat. A Nazi soldier stood behind him. Then the world shifted, and the Nazi snapped into the form of a young British corporal. Major Granville's corporal.

"Mr. Merrin," the man said. "The major will see you, sir."

Merrin forced himself to breathe. "Thank you."

The corporal ushered Merrin into Major Granville's office. The major sat behind his desk like a baron in a fortress. Merrin tucked the leather case under his arm and felt his stomach grow tight with tension. "Baron" was the perfect word. Granville ran this district of Kenya like a fiefdom, dividing up coffee farms and tea groves among his countrymen like a lord handing down inheritances, with no regard that the natives had owned them first.

Despite the fact that it had lost millions of pounds in the early days, England had never lost interest in colonizing Africa. In 1890, it reached a final agreement with Germany, giving the Kaiser control over what would one day become Tanzania while England took over a section farther northwest and renamed it Kenya. The natives who already occupied the territories in question were not consulted. Territorial lines were drawn without regard to local custom, and in more than one case, entire villages were split in half.

The Imperial British East Africa Company tried to run the new colony and failed miserably, losing millions and forcing the British government to take over in 1895. To bring the natives under control, the new governor pitted rival groups against each other, setting the drought-and-famine-ridden Masai against their wealthier neighbors in a classic divide-and-conquer tactic. Families and villages were shattered by tribal warfare, and the colonial government eagerly snapped up the pieces.

None of this had been accepted easily by the native tribes. Not a year went by that some group or other didn't try to shake off British shackles. But the British were better armed and better organized and they always smashed rebellions flat. Merrin, however, was already wondering how much longer this could go on. The tribes were starting to see through the divide-and-conquer trick, and the wind whispered rumors of dark-skinned Africans setting aside tribal differences to fight the hated white-skinned British.

The hated white-skinned British, in this particular case, was Major Granville. From the native perspective, he lived in luxury, with steady electricity, fine clothes, and fine food. His men collected stiff taxes and high rents. When people couldn't pay, Granville conscripted them into the British army as servants and cooks. He seized land and crops, leaving the former owners starving and destitute. And when they came to him to beg for food, he slammed them into service contracts that stole their freedom. It made Merrin's blood boil to see it. Merrin, however, had learned the hard way that resistance against such people was fruitless, even dangerous.

It was easier to hide in the world of scholarship and archaeology.

Beside the major stood a younger man wearing a Roman collar. The other priest had a slender build and a narrow face topped by thick brown hair. Merrin didn't recognize him. What was going on here?

"Father Merrin," the strange priest said, offering a hand. "I'm Father Will Francis."

Merrin felt a little nonplused, but gave a warm hand-shake that left dry dust on the other man's palm. "Nice to meet you."

"And this is Major Granville, of course."

Merrin gave a curt nod. "Major."

"Your cable couldn't have come at a better time, sir. Glad to see you've arrived safely. Drink?" Granville held up a glass, and Merrin noticed there was a large blue butterfly in a jar on the man's desk. A wet cotton ball lay in the bottom of the jar, and Merrin caught a faint whiff of ether. The smell put him off the idea of a drink. The butterfly inside beat its wings against the glass like a pan-icked fairy.

"No, thank you, Major."

"As you like," Granville said, and handed the glass to Francis, who accepted it with a startled look. The motion was reflected in the glass of the butterfly cases, and Merrin automatically looked to them. Granville noticed.

"Beautiful, aren't they?" he said.

"Very," Merrin replied. "I didn't know you were a lep-idopterist."

Granville raised gray eyebrows. "You know the correct term. I suppose I shouldn't be surprised." He raised his glass at the collection. The butterflies sat perfectly motionless behind their panes of glass, in stark contrast to their struggling brother. "I've picked up a few new ones in my tour here."

Merrin leaned closer to examine one specimen. Bright orange wings, wide black stripes. The label below it read: CALLIORATIS MILLARI: SOUTH AFRICA. Merrin caught his breath.

"A South African tiger moth," he said. "They haven't been seen in South Africa for over twenty-five years."

"I know," the major said, looking pleased. "I captured one of the last living specimens. Extraordinary, isn't it?"

"Truly," Merrin murmured, though it came out as a growl. The blue butterfly's movements grew weaker.

"It's a hobby from my school days." Granville took a long sip of whiskey. "It does wonders for the nerves. You should try it sometime."

"I have a hobby," Merrin said.

"Archaeology?" Francis said. He was holding his glass by the rim as if he thought it might explode. "That's hardly a hobby for someone like you."

"For someone like me," Merrin replied, "that's all it can be. What can you tell me about this dig?"

Granville nodded. "The location is a remote area of the Turkana region called Derati. A garrison of my men discovered the structure while on maneuvers there several months ago. When the powers that be realized its importance, a dig was organized."

"What powers that be?" Merrin asked, though deep down he already knew the answer.

"Rome," Father Francis put in. "The building is clearly a church, and the Vatican wants it dealt with properly."

"Even though it's a church where no church should be," Merrin said.

"*Especially* because it's a church where no church should be," Francis asserted.

"So who is funding the dig?" Merrin asked.

"It's a joint venture," Granville replied, "between the Vatican and the Crown."

"Really?" Merrin said, eyebrows raised. "I didn't know the British government had that kind of relationship with the Vatican."

"We don't—officially," Granville said. "Officially all the money comes from the Vatican by way of Cardinal Jenkins here in Nairobi. The Crown, however, has made a great many supplies available to the dig. Unofficially."

"So tell me, do you have any theories on who might have built this church?" Francis said a little too eagerly. He reminded Merrin of a puppy trying to behave itself in the presence of an older, more dignified dog.

"Not until I see it," he said. "But surely the Vatican has a record of its creation."

Francis shook his head. "I'm afraid not. We're as much in the dark about it as you are."

"How do you know it's a Christian church and not some other structure?" Merrin suggested. "A pre-Christian temple, for example?"

"Enough of it has been exposed to tell us otherwise," Francis said. He was still holding the whiskey glass. "It's clearly Christian Byzantine. No question."

"It still shouldn't be there," Merrin mused aloud, becoming more intrigued despite his attempts to remain aloof. "Christian missionaries didn't arrive in this part of Africa until fairly recently, and there has been no major Catholic presence until this past decade. The Church—capital C—certainly hasn't been around long enough to leave an archaeological record."

The butterfly dropped to the bottom of the jar and went completely still. Granville tapped the lid, but it didn't respond. "Our thinking exactly. I was very glad to receive the wire saying you were volunteering to take over the dig. We were at a bit of a loss—qualified archae-ologists aren't easy to come by in this part of the world. Cardinal Jenkins wanted the dig to continue, and it has, but without proper supervision."

Granville's words brought another pang to Merrin's stomach. He was seized with the urge to run out the door and straight down to the dig site before more dam-age could be done. "Have you been to the site, Father Francis?" he asked instead.

"No," Francis replied. "I've only read the reports."

"Then what is your capacity here?"

"Him?" Granville looked up from the dead butterfly, surprised. "Well, for one thing he's quite an admirer of yours, and he asked—"

Francis set his untouched whiskey on Granville's desk. "I'm about to begin missionary work in the Turkana district, Father Merrin." He cleared his throat. "This is a little awkward. Cardinal Jenkins is some-what . . . concerned about an exploration of this signifi-cance being conducted by a priest on . . . on sabbatical.

The cardinal wants a Church representative on site at the dig."

"Oh?" Merrin said, liking the situation less and less. "In what capacity?"

"Just as an observer for the Church," Francis said hurriedly. "In addition to my missionary work. I need to make sure that any holy relics are treated properly."

"The Church doesn't trust me to do it?" Merrin asked. "No, don't answer that, Father. I know what the Vatican thinks of me."

"They think you're the best archaeologist ever to complete seminary," Francis said stoutly. "I have to say it's a pleasure to meet you, Father Merrin. I've read all your work."

"It's Mister Merrin."

The reply made Francis falter. "Of course. Er . . . I was especially impressed with your treatise on the Roman rituals. Tell me, have you heard the rumors of their revision?"

"I'm afraid I'm no longer privy to those discussions, Father." Merrin leaned one hand on Granville's desk. "But surely you didn't come all this way to discuss archaic Catholic rituals."

Francis gave a small laugh. "No. I was actually headed to Kenya to begin missionary work when Rome learned of the discovery. As I said, they've asked me to make sure the site's religious aspects are given proper consideration."

"Are you an archaeologist, Father Francis?"

"I . . . have my degree," Francis said evasively.

"How many digs have you been on?"

"Two. One in Jerusalem and one in Egypt."

"When you were a seminary student?"

". . . Yes."

"How many digs have you overseen?"

Francis hesitated. "Technically, none. Though I was second assistant on the Jerusalem dig."

Merrin narrowed his eyes. Experience had taught him that "observers" usually tried to poke their noses into parts of the dig where they only made trouble, and it was obvious that this boy barely knew one end of a trowel from the other. One mistake could destroy priceless information forever. Even experts made their fair share of errors, and they knew what they were doing. Putting an inexperienced digger in charge of a major find was like handing a Ming vase to a toddler. Will Francis seemed nice enough, but who knew what the man would be like when they got to the site?

Granville, meanwhile, unscrewed the jar lid and eased the blue butterfly out onto his desk. From a drawer he took a mounting board and a box of pins. Merrin's stomach turned. He didn't want to watch what was coming next.

"I suppose we should get on our way, then," Merrin said. "The sooner, the better."

"Of course," Granville agreed, not looking up from the butterfly. "Chuma, your foreman, is waiting out back with a lorry. When you get to Derati, you'll want to talk to Trenton Jefferies. He was the only white man working at the dig when the previous chief archaeologist left, and I asked him to keep an eye on things until we could find a replacement."

"And where do I find this Mr. Jefferies?" Merrin asked.

"From what I hear tell, if he's not at the dig, he holes up in the local bar. Good luck, and keep me apprised."

Merrin thanked the major and left, with Francis trailing after him like a lost duckling.

Three

✠

Turkana, British East Africa

It is not right to beat the messenger.
—Kenyan proverb

A TWO-VEHICLE CONVOY crawled slowly over East African terrain. The rich vegetation and red earth surrounding the frosty peaks of Mount Kenya gave way to rough black hills to the north. The hills grew flatter and more barren until they disappeared entirely, swallowed up by the sandy plains of Turkana.

Although Turkana was a desert, it wasn't filled with blowing sand and featureless dunes. Acacia trees dotted a landscape of rocky, scrubby hills, canyons, and dry riverbeds lined with palm trees. The convoy had found one of the latter and was using it as a handy natural highway.

The second vehicle was a Rover. The first was an

ancient lorry filled with supplies and people, a good half of whom were native hitchhikers picked up along the way. Will Francis, seated in the Rover, had initially fumed at the delay created every time the little convoy stopped to pick up someone new; he was eager to reach the site and see this impossible church. But Merrin, who seemed to know a great many African customs, had tersely explained that cars and lorries were rare in Africa, and it was considered the height of rudeness to refuse anyone in need of transportation.

"If you want to play missionary to these people," he had firmly suggested, "you should keep your mouth shut until you understand their customs. Otherwise you're going to spend most of your time tasting your own feet."

Will had started to argue, but then he saw the wisdom in Merrin's words. Offended people wouldn't hear his words, or God's. So Will said nothing. Instead, he turned his attention to the hitchhikers in the lorry ahead of him. Many of them wore western dress, but equally many were dressed in the bright colors of their native land. The women in native garb wore long shoulderless dresses that shone like rainbows while the men wore bright red wraps that covered them from waist to knee. The other men wore tattered khaki brown explorer shirts. None of the women, Will noticed, wore western clothing. At least they didn't seem to be immodest. Will had, of course, heard stories about bare-breasted jungle women, but he hadn't yet seen any. He wasn't sure whether to be relieved or disappointed. With a pang, he sent up a quick prayer for for-

32

giveness and added it to his mental tally of sins to confess later.

Abruptly it occurred to him that there would be no one to hear his confessions. He himself was, of course, empowered to hear confessions and assign penance, but who would hear his own? With Merrin's status uncertain, Will wasn't sure the other man was able to grant any kind of absolution. What if something happened out here in the middle of nowhere and he died without absolution or last rites? Accidents happened all the time. Will swallowed, then forced himself to think rationally. God wouldn't have sent him out here without a safety net. God wouldn't let him die without absolution. He had only to trust in God.

The thought made him feel a little better as the lorry jolted across the uneven riverbed. Will clung to the door handle with grim determination. He was going to be sore tomorrow, he could tell already. The terrain just wasn't made for driving. The Rover jolted over sand and stone, kicking up a cloud of dust. More dust from the lorry ahead caked in Will's throat and itched on his skin. They were almost to the site, and every so often the riverbed walls fell away, revealing the sparkling waters of Lake Rudolf on the horizon to Will's left. To his right lay a series of low hills.

Merrin was making the trip north in cold silence, speaking only when necessary. Will felt disappointed. Lankester Merrin was one of the great archaeological minds of the twentieth century, and Will had been looking forward to talking to him. As a seminary student, he had read everything Merrin had written, even done two papers on Merrin's findings. Now he was sitting in the presence of the man himself, and Merrin didn't want to talk to him.

Will grimaced. He couldn't really blame Merrin. Will had to look like an interloper, swooping in and taking over. To tell the truth, he was nervous. No, he was *terrified*. He had a degree in archaeology, had been on one dig in Jerusalem and one in Egypt. But he had never actually been in charge of a project before, and certainly not one of this magnitude. Cardinal Jenkins, however, had insisted. Will was the only priest in Africa who had an archaeological background and who could get to the dig in time to ensure the Church's interests. And although Lankester Merrin may have been a renowned archaeologist, he wasn't, of late, a very good priest.

Chuma maneuvered the Rover around a large boulder. He was a tall, powerful Kenyan with small eyes and an expansive expression. Chuma, Will had decided early on, was a people person, good at talking, good at listening—and apparently the biggest gossip in all Kenya.

". . . and that is why my uncle can no longer have children," Chuma said, gesturing at the people in the lorry ahead of them. "Now Odaka—he is the one talking to my second cousin Kulu on the left side of the lorry— Odaka thinks we of his family do not know about his mistress. He also thinks his wife knows nothing of her, but of course she does."

"Adultery is a sin," Will said, feeling obliged to point this out. "Why does the community tolerate it?"

"For her sake, of course. If Tula, his wife, wished it exposed, she would expose it. We remain silent so she will not be embarrassed. And of course I have been trying to convince Odaka to do the right thing."

"End the affair?" Will said.

"Take his mistress as a second wife," Chuma corrected.

"Of course," Will murmured, realizing his missionary work had been cut out for him. He couldn't help asking, "Why doesn't Odaka take his mistress as a second wife?"

Chuma looked surprised. "Because Tula would never allow it."

The Rover hit a particularly hard bump, and Will nearly banged his head into the ceiling. Grimacing, he caught a glimpse of a small smile beneath Merrin's hat. Because of the bump or because of Chuma's remark? Maybe it was both.

"So the mines are in the hills?" Will said in a change of subject, gesturing out the open window.

"*Were*," Chuma answered. His English was British and perfect. "They are all closed down now. Derati was quite a boom town once. Gold—that's what brought the British here."

"That," Merrin chimed in, "and a cheap source of labor."

"What do you mean?" Will asked.

Merrin gave him a hard look. "If you want to be a good archaeologist, Francis, you should do your research," he said flatly. "I did. The discovery of gold in Derati touched off a sensation in British circles. But they needed someone to mine it. Getting their own hands dirty was out of the question, so naturally they turned to the 'lesser people.' " Merrin's lip curled at the last phrase. "However, even the British balked at conscripting laborers out of the blue. There had to be a *reason* to snatch them up. Fortunately for the British, they had Major Granville."

"I don't understand," Will said.

"Granville is in charge of the province around Derati. He declared that the gold deposits increased the value of the land tenfold, and he levied new taxes accordingly. Within a month, every native inhabitant of Derati defaulted his land. Entire families, including children as young as *five*, were conscripted to work in the new mines to pay off the new tax debt. Think of it, Father. Small children forced underground to work the mines for twelve hours a day. And every penny went straight to Granville's office."

Will pursed his lips. "I see."

"It gets better," Merrin continued. "The people revolted three times, and all three times Granville's men smashed them down. Then the gold gave out. The British disappeared, leaving behind impoverished people and poisoned wells. And they've done nothing to help these people since. Perhaps now, Father, you can understand why I was less than enthusiastic about British and Vatican involvement in this discovery, whatever it turns out to be."

In the lorry ahead of them, someone said something funny, and all the passengers burst out laughing, a strange counterpoint to the serious conversation in the Rover.

"You were a foreman at the mine?" Will Francis said to Chuma.

The man nodded. "It was where I learned English."

"How long have you been with the dig?" Merrin asked.

"Since it began. The British brought me in as an interpreter."

"What's Derati like now? Do you have a source of income or trade?"

"We raise goats and cows and camels," Chuma said. "And there are the wells. Before the mines, traders came to Derati for the water. They still do, but several of the wells were poisoned by the mining, so not as many come as once did."

"Don't your people get water from the lake?" Will asked in surprise.

"The lake has always been brackish. It is a hard life, but we make do as best we can."

A tense silence fell on the Rover after that. An hour later, the miniature convoy left the riverbed and came to a halt at the outskirts of Derati. Merrin, Chuma, and Will all climbed down from the Rover, stretching their legs and arms after the long ride. Will beat some of the dust from the khakis he wore over his collar. A hot sun burned overhead, and the air lay perfectly still, like held breath. Ahead of them, the hitchhikers clambered down from the lorry. Will looked around, squinting in the harsh African sunlight.

The village outskirts consisted of a series of beehive-shaped huts made of mud and brown palm fronds woven over wooden frames. Will, however, could see the roofs of European-style brick and plaster buildings poking up inside the outer circle of huts. A squad of naked and near-naked children dashed out from the village to see who had arrived. They surrounded Merrin like a flock of chattering birds. Merrin smiled at them and dug a handful of sweets from his pockets for general distribution. Each child got two—one for now and one to save. They ran off in a shrieking pack, comparing the brightly colored bits of hard candy as if they were valued jewels.

"How did you know to do that?" Will asked. "Have you been here before?"

"I've been to Ethiopia," Merrin said, "but it's the same everywhere—the children like sweets and the parents like people who are nice to the children. Something for you to remember next time."

"So why are we stopping? We aren't in town yet."

Merrin gestured toward the hitchhikers, most of whom were staring at something off to one side. "I think they want to watch."

Will shaded his eyes in an attempt to follow their gaze when an enraged bellow brought his head around and he saw what everyone was looking at.

In a nearby field stood a group of Turkana tribesmen, all dressed in long red sarongs. They were circling a full-grown black bull tied to a stake driven deep into the rocky ground. Red designs had been painted on the animal's hide, and its horns were tipped with gold. The men carried long spears decorated with bright paint, beads, and feathers. They danced around the animal, feinting at it in a ritual pattern. One man, slightly taller than the rest and wearing an elaborate headdress that spread like a peacock's tail, stood to one side with his arms folded across his bare chest.

Abruptly one of the men thrust his spear deep into the bull's flank. It bellowed in rage and pain and whipped its head around to gore its attacker, but the man had already danced out of the way. Once the bull's attention was distracted, another man slipped in and speared it a second time.

Will stared in shock and horror as the bull bawled and snorted red foam. "Why are they tormenting that animal?" he demanded.

"It is a sacrifice," Chuma said. "The new wife of our chief elder, Sebituana, will soon give birth. So the people make sacrifices in the hope that the gods will provide a male heir." He noticed Will's aghast expression and turned to face him. "You think we are savages."

"No. Simply good people lost in confusion," Will said carefully.

Merrin squinted idly up at the sky. "That's the problem with missionaries. They confuse difference with ignorance."

"Brutality is *always* ignorance, Father Merrin," Will countered before he could stop himself. "You of all people should know that."

Merrin looked at him and Will braced himself for a verbal onslaught. Even though he firmly believed he was right, being castigated by Lankester Merrin would not be pleasant. But to his surprise, Merrin stared for a moment, then simply nodded.

The bull bellowed again. Blood flowed from the panting animal's nose. For a moment, Will seriously considered running over and yanking the spears from the Turkana's hands, then realized as quickly that it would accomplish nothing and probably make the people angry to boot. And angry people wouldn't listen to God's word. Best to keep silent for now. He couldn't prevent this cruelty, but he might prevent it from happening again.

Another thrust, another bellow, and the bull's front legs buckled. One of the tribesmen, a tall and impressive man, leaped onto the back of the animal's neck with a machete. In a lightning movement, he whipped it down and across the bull's throat. The beast crashed to the ground as the machete wielder danced free. The man in the headdress—Sebituana—nodded his praise. Two more men ran forward bearing an earthenware trough. They held it under the ghastly wound and caught the steaming rush of blood. Will felt sick. He turned to Chuma and asked, "You can't believe in these superstitions, can you?"

"I believe that we have much to learn from the whites," Chuma said with great diplomacy.

"And your countrymen?" Will nodded toward the men with the bloody trough.

"They," Chuma said gravely, "believe that you bring trouble."

"What the hell?" Merrin muttered, striding away before either of the other men could react. Will scrambled to follow, with Chuma bringing up the rear. They covered fifty or sixty yards before they caught up with Merrin, whose eyes were now transfixed by something on the ground.

"What is it?" Will demanded. "What's wr—"

Will stopped beside Merrin, now seeing what had caught his colleague's attention. In a slight hollow in the ground before them lay row upon row of white stone crosses. Hundreds of them. They stretched across the hollow like giant snowflakes. Merrin adjusted his hat, clearly uncomfortable. Will swallowed.

"What happened here, Chuma?" Merrin asked.

"A plague," the foreman replied matter-of-factly. "It ravaged this valley fifty years ago."

"How many died?"

Chuma shrugged. "All of them."

"We should get back to the lorry," Will advised. "Someone might . . . I mean, the equipment . . ."

"You fear the villagers will steal from you," Chuma said. Before Will could protest, he continued. "It is a legitimate concern. Many people are poor these days."

"When you say, 'all of them,' Chuma," Merrin said as they headed back to the lorry, "were you being rhetorical? That old riddle—where did they bury the survivors?"

"No." Chuma wiped sweat from his forehead with his sleeves. "I mean everyone died. The plague killed the entire village."

"Why are they buried in Christian graves?" Merrin asked. "I thought Christianity had nothing more than a toehold here, and then only recently."

"Not quite true," Will put in. "We've had missionaries in this area for a long time. The Church's influence was pretty strong a while ago. Derati used to be very Christian in the years before the gold rush."

"And how do you know that?"

"If you want to be a good archaeologist, Merrin, you should do your research," Will said blandly. "*I* did."

Merrin snorted. Will couldn't tell if it was a good snort or a bad one, so he decided to take it as a good sign.

As they reached the lorry, Will saw that most of the hitchhikers had gathered around the men who were butchering the carcass of the bull. Flies were already swarming in a thick cloud, and one of the older warriors was handing enormous green leaves to some of the nearby children, clearly instructing them to use the leaves as fans to keep the insects from settling. The chatter of foreign language and the buzz of angry flies filled Will's ears. The buzzing grew louder as he approached the lorry.

"The Church didn't keep records about Derati during the gold rush," he continued, raising his voice slightly. "But Cardinal Jenkins had the journals of some of the missionaries who worked here near the turn of the century. I read them before we left."

"So everyone died in the plague," Merrin said, climbing into the cab. Several hitchhikers leaped into the back. "And without the firm, guiding hand of the missionaries, the place reverted back to its pagan roots. Guess the Church wasn't as strong as it thought."

The remark needled Will, whose nerves were already shortened by the long and tiring journey. "We'll see what we can do to change that," he said shortly.

"Bit of a temper," Merrin said as he scooted into the Rover beside Will. "Good. I was afraid you were one of those annoying priests who's always sappy and serene."

Chuma started the Rover, which only reluctantly ground to life. Will didn't know what to say to Merrin's remark, so he remained silent as they left the dead bull and white crosses behind to drive into the village proper.

The village of Derati was pretty much what Merrin had been expecting—a boom town gone to seed. Once they cleared the outer ring of low, thatched mud huts, they encountered European brick and plaster buildings. Chuma drove them into a town center complete with a main street and a square. Shops, restaurants, and bars that at one time catered to mine workers and their British overseers now catered to nobody. Most of the buildings were boarded up, and the boardwalk had sagged and cracked. Rain and sun had beaten the white-washed buildings gray. Children played in the streets, forcing Chuma and the truck driver ahead to slow to a crawl as they reached the square. Women spread wares to sell on blankets, and a scattering of shoppers, both European and African, browsed through them. A white man in a pith helmet with a rifle on his back trooped up the boardwalk followed by two natives carrying yellow bundles of ivory tusks on their heads like firewood. Blood still stained the ends. An Indian merchant stood outside his store, watching the Rover and lorry with idle interest.

As the vehicles came to a halt, a European woman stepped from the doorway of another building. Her shoulder-length blond hair was pulled back into a practical French braid, and she wore a doctor's field kit. A stethoscope dangled from her neck. She was wiping her hands on a white towel. Behind her came a native boy, seven or eight years old, if Merrin was any judge. About the same age as the boy who had sold him the Anubis puppet in Cairo. He had short brown hair, long, skinny arms, and a solemn face.

Merrin climbed down from the Rover a second time, with a pair of small, weather-beaten suitcases in his hands. Although he technically didn't need to keep his onetime vow of poverty anymore, money hadn't exactly been falling into his pockets since the war, and he had few possessions. He made a wry face. At least poverty—whatever its source—let you travel light. He stretched again, glad after three days to be standing on something that didn't bounce, jolt, or bump.

The lorry, meanwhile, shed hitchhikers like autumn leaves. The children had reappeared, scampering around the little convoy, puppies around a mother dog. Merrin watched the European woman approach, still holding her towel. She was very pretty, with a wide smile and sky-blue eyes. He found it surprisingly hard to take his gaze off her.

That's another vow you don't need to keep, murmured an inner voice. Merrin told it to shut the hell up.

The woman nodded briefly at Merrin and Will, then headed straight for Chuma. "Welcome back," she said, shaking his hand. "Did you bring the supplies?"

"They are in the lorry," Chuma said. "Everything you asked for. Joseph, take Dr. Novack's supplies inside for her."

44

Joseph, the young boy, nodded and dashed to the rear of the lorry. Since it was apparent the woman had no intention of introducing herself, Merrin set down his suitcases and stepped forward, hand outstretched. "I'm Lankester Merrin. This is Father Will Francis."

"Dr. Sarah Novack," she said, returning the handshake.

"A woman doctor?" Will asked, eyebrows raised.

"I get very tired of hearing that," Sarah sighed. She had a Polish accent. "Yes, Father, I am a doctor. Yes, I attended medical school. Yes, I practice real medicine. Yes, with real patients. No, they do not die more often than anyone else's patients. No, I do not just handle pregnancy and pediatrics."

"Uh, sorry," he said, cheeks flushing.

"You're here to take over the dig, Mr. Merrin?" Sarah asked.

"Yes, with Father Francis. He'll be keeping an eye on Church interests."

"I see." She turned to Chuma again. "Chuma, was there any mail for me?"

Chuma handed her a single envelope from his breast pocket, then told Merrin, "There is only one hotel in Derati. You can also eat and drink there. Please come this way." He strode off.

Merrin threw Sarah an apologetic glance. Her face was completely neutral, as if she hadn't decided yet whether to like him or not. At least she didn't seem to hate him. For some reason, that felt dreadfully important to Merrin. He caught up his suitcases and followed Chuma, with Will once again trailing behind. The priest carried two suitcases as well, one of which appeared to be very heavy. Merrin wondered if it was full of books—Bibles for the Derati, or something.

Chuma had already reached the boardwalk and was entering a door beneath a sign that read EMEKWI'S BAR AND HOTEL in uneven handwriting. Merrin followed him inside, and felt as if he'd been struck blind. The interior was black as a grave after the harsh light outside. The place smelled of stale beer, and the air was rather cooler than outdoors. As Merrin's vision adjusted, he made out a few figures sitting among wooden tables and a few more seated at a long bar. He took off his hat.

Behind the bar stood a large African man dressed in western clothes. A twelve-year-old African boy was sweeping the floor while the barman rinsed glasses in a basin of water. He looked up when the three men entered, and a smile burst across his face. The boy stopped sweeping to stare at the newcomers.

"*Harabi*, Chuma," the man said, "and also to you, gentlemen! It's always a fine thing to see new faces in my hotel. Do you need rooms?"

"Eventually," Merrin said. "Right now I'm looking for Trenton Jefferies."

"He is in the corner behind you, sir," the barman said.

Merrin turned. Shadows clumped around a corner table, and Merrin could barely see the man occupying it. Merrin set his bags by the door and approached, not bothering to check for Will Francis to follow. He put out his hand.

"I'm Lankester Merrin, the new chief archaeologist.

Major Granville said you've been in charge of the dig since the first archaeologist left?"

Jefferies leaned forward to shake Merrin's hand, and his face came into the light. Merrin froze. The man's face was covered with boils as large and red as wine grapes. Some of them leaked yellow-green pus. Merrin thought he caught the smell of rotten meat. His stomach made a slow, nauseating twist.

"Something bothering you, mate?" Jefferies asked.

Merrin came to himself. "No," he said blandly, and took back his hand. There was a beat, then Jefferies gestured at Merrin to sit. Merrin hung his hat on the back of the chair and obeyed, trying to keep polite eye contact without staring. On the table in front of Jefferies was a bottle of scotch and a single glass.

"Long trip?" Jefferies asked.

"Cairo," Merrin said, "then Nairobi. I feel like I've been traveling for years."

"Sounds like you need something to wash the dust out of your throat, then," Jefferies said. "You drink, Merrin?"

"I shouldn't." Merrin looked long and hard at the bottle. Amber liquid rippled enticingly inside. "But my will is weak."

A grin crawled across Jefferies's face like a spider. A boil on his cheek split, and clear liquid trickled into his collar. Jefferies didn't seem to notice. "Then you might just survive this place."

He filled his glass with scotch and pushed it across the table to Merrin, then took a swig directly from the bottle. Merrin thought about where the glass had been and had to force himself to pick it up. A dead fly was floating in the scotch. Merrin's stomach turned again. He brought the glass to his lips and pretended to sip.

"I understand you've uncovered the church dome, but progress has slowed a little."

"You could say that," Jefferies replied, looking past Merrin. "Right, Doctor?"

Merrin turned. Sarah Novack was standing in the bar doorway talking to Will Francis. She looked at Jefferies when he said her name. "What's that?"

Jefferies raised the bottle to her. "You still haven't made it by my room, Doc. I've been having a little swelling in the evening. Perhaps you have something I can put on it?"

"How about a muzzle?" Sarah said. "Or I could lance it for you."

Jefferies guffawed and took another swig. Merrin ran his glass over the tabletop. The fly sloshed around, caught in the waves of scotch. Was it kicking? He cleared his throat.

"So how are the interior excavations coming on?" he asked.

"They're not," Jefferies said, his eyes still on Sarah.

Merrin looked surprised. "Has the structure collapsed?"

"No, the church is perfect so far. But none of the men will enter. The ones we have left, anyway." He drained the rest of the bottle and gave a small belch. Merrin smelled a warm puff of scotch. "I'm leaving for the dig in five minutes if you want to come along. It's only a short drive away."

He rose from the table, gave Sarah one last look, then stumbled out the door. The moment he was gone, Sarah sat down in the chair he had occupied. Francis and Chuma were talking to the bartender.

"Pleasant fellow, that Jefferies," Merrin said, gladder than he should have been that Sarah was now sitting across from him. "What's wrong with his face?"

"Other than that it's attached to his head?" Sarah growled. "Actually, I'm not sure what the problem is. Every time he comes in for an examination, he drools and asks if I want to undress him, so I haven't been able to give him a good going-over. It could be an allergic reaction or some kind of localized infection."

"I suppose I should feel sorry for him." Merrin raised his hand to the bartender and mouthed "Beer?" at him. "What are you having?"

"Sobriety," Sarah said. "I drank a lifetime of gin just after the War. Not," she added quickly, "that I think everyone else should abstain."

Merrin smiled. He was smiling at a pretty woman, something he hadn't done in a long time. He found he liked it. After a moment he realized neither of them had spoken for quite some time. He cleared his throat.

"So why won't the men enter the church?" he asked.

Sarah shrugged. "Evil spirits. If you believe the Turkana."

"And do you?"

"Hardly. I'm a doctor." She laughed. "But as a priest, surely you must believe in such things."

"I'm an archaeologist, Doctor, not a priest."

Sarah tilted her head becomingly. "That's funny. I was just talking to Father Francis over there, and he said you were."

"Did he?" Merrin felt his earlier irritation rise again. "Well, he's mistaken."

"Doctor! Dr. Novack!" Joseph, the solemn-faced boy who had met the lorry, dashed into the bar. "I put your boxes in the clinic."

"Thank you, Joseph," Sarah said warmly. "You're a good helper."

"I'm going to be a doctor, too," Joseph told Merrin. "Dr. Novack's going to help me."

"Then you'll probably be the best doctor in the world," Merrin said.

Joseph grinned shyly. He turned to rush away, and almost barreled into Father Francis and the bartender, who had come over to the table. The bartender put a hand on Joseph's shoulder to steady him.

"Be careful," he admonished. "Doctors heal. They don't harm."

"This is my father," Joseph said. "But I don't know your name."

"You can call me *Mister* Merrin," he answered with a hard look at Will Francis, who had the grace to flush. "I'm going to be working at the dig."

"This is Emekwi," Francis said, gesturing at the bartender. "He's donating the use of a room here in the hotel for the mission school."

Emekwi set a beer bottle on the table and reached down to pump Merrin's hand enthusiastically. "We're so glad you're here. As he said, I am Emekwi, owner of this bar and the hotel attached to it, and this is my son Joseph. My other son"—he nodded at the older boy who was sweeping the floor—"is James. They are learning the Bible." He leaned forward with an enormous white grin. "We are Christians, you know."

"I'm sure Father Francis is pleased," Merrin said, carefully neutral.

A horn honked impatiently from outside, and a small rhesus monkey raced into the bar. It shot across the floor and scampered up to James's shoulder. The boy paused in his sweeping long enough to pet the animal before going back to work.

"That would be our Mr. Jefferies," Sarah said.

"The monkey?" Merrin said with a straight face.

Sarah aimed a mock slap at his shoulder. "In the jeep outside. Emekwi, Mr. Merrin has to go. Can you see to his bags?"

"Of course," Emekwi said. "James! Joseph!"

James hurried over to Merrin's suitcases and hoisted one with some effort. The monkey made a small screech of protest. Joseph, however, moved toward Merrin.

"What do you do best?" he asked.

Surprised, Merrin thought a moment. "I dig a nice hole."

"Why would you want to dig a hole?"

"To see what's inside," Merrin told him. "Sometimes you can find little pieces of history."

"Is it like rock collecting?" Joseph asked.

Merrin smiled. "Exactly."

Another impatient honk from outside. Merrin rose

and shook Emekwi's hand. "I'm afraid I'll have to put the beer off until later," he said, and turned to Sarah. "Doctor, it was nice . . ."

He trailed off and stared at a fly crawling around the edge of his abandoned glass. The insect shook its wings in a tiny spray of scotch, rose from the glass, and buzzed away.

"Mr. Merrin?" Sarah said in a tone that hinted . . . concern?

Merrin shook his head. Outside, the horn honked a third time. "Sorry. It's been a strange day. Very nice to meet you, Dr. Novack."

Without turning to see if Francis was following, he said gruffly, "Father. Shall we?" He snatched up his hat and strode out the door.

The harsh afternoon sunlight slammed into Merrin, and he hurriedly clapped his hat on. It was still roasting hot outside, and it dawned on him that he hadn't actually had anything to drink in the bar. Maybe Jefferies would have a canteen. Then Merrin shuddered. Better to stay thirsty until they reached the site before sharing a water container with Jefferies.

Jefferies, meanwhile, sat with obvious impatience in a scruffy Rover parked in front of the bar. Behind it was the lorry, with Chuma at the wheel. It still contained supplies for the dig, fresh from Nairobi.

"You ready, mate?" Jefferies shouted. His face looked all the more horrific in the sunlight. Some of his boils were large enough to cast sharp shadows, and Merrin could see every pustule with perfect clarity.

"Ready." Merrin climbed into the passenger seat.

Francis, who had indeed followed him, got quietly in the back.

As Jefferies drove the Rover through the town with the lorry behind, Francis finally said to Merrin, "I really didn't ask for this, you know. I know I'm not very experienced and that this is your dig. You must be . . . unhappy with the cardinal—and with me."

"You're here," Merrin replied. "The cardinal isn't."

"Right. Anyway, I want you to know that I'm not planning on taking over in any real sense. I'll be the official head, meaning I'll sign paperwork and make reports to Major Granville and the cardinal, but I won't touch anything you don't want me to. I won't even *breathe* around the dig without your permission."

They reached the edge of town and continued down a rutted, dusty road that wound among low hills covered with scrubby vegetation. Herds of goats tended by young boys browsed among the leaves and bushes. Overhead, the sun continued to burn with heavy, golden heat. Jefferies drove in silence. Merrin turned in his seat to look at Francis. "And what about the rest of it?"

"Rest of what?" Francis asked, confused.

"My position and title." He leaned further toward Francis. "In case I wasn't clear earlier, I. Am. Not. A. Priest."

"You're on temporary sabbatical," Father Francis pointed out with infuriating calm. He seemed to have gotten over his earlier awe of him, Merrin noticed, disgruntled. "You haven't officially left the Church. That means you're *still* a priest."

"You sound like a Jesuit," Merrin said.

"Maryknoll, actually."

"I'm done with being a priest, Francis."

"Then why haven't you resigned?"

The question hung between them, suspended on harsh beams of sunlight, and Merrin's mind chewed on it like a bulldog. *Because the War closed a dozen doors on me and I don't want to close another one if I don't have to. Because not quite resigning makes the Church wait on my terms. Because I don't want to see "I told you so" looks on anyone's faces if I opt for reinstatement.*

"Because," was all he said.

"Have you broken any of your priestly vows?" Francis persisted.

Merrin thought about Sarah. "Other than not going to confession in a while, no."

"Have you submitted your resignation to an archbishop? Have you petitioned the Holy Father to let you join the laity?"

"No, but—"

"Then in the eyes of God and the Church, you're still a priest."

"This isn't an argument you can win with ecclesiastic hand waving and Maryknoll logic, Francis," Merrin snapped. "God and the Church—" He cut himself off.

"God and the Church what?" Francis asked.

—abandoned me. "Nothing. I'm not a priest, Francis, and I'd appreciate it if you'd stop telling people that I am."

"That's the way to tell him, mate!" Jefferies chimed in. "What's the fun in being a priest, anyway? You can't shag anyone—or even wank it. 'Course, that ain't stopped a fair number of priests, has it?" He roared at his own joke. Francis fell silent, for which Merrin was grateful.

The Rover wound its way out of the hills and toward a rocky plain. The waters of Lake Rudolf glittered at the horizon, and Merrin caught the metallic scent of brackish water. Rocky desert dotted with stubborn bushes stretched in all other directions.

Jefferies guided the Rover down toward a pair of brown hills with a shallow ravine between them. As they grew closer, Merrin spotted the dig site. It sat on a flat spot between the upper rises of the two hills. Like all the other digs Merrin had supervised, the place sported a grid marked with low stakes and white string. A clump of nearby tents provided office space, and dark-skinned workers bustled about with baskets, trowels, brushes, and other tools.

Merrin's eye, however, was drawn to the structure. It stuck out of the ground at the eastern end of the dig and, as Jefferies had said, did indeed appear to be the corner of a roof. He saw an eave and what seemed to be the upper portion of a wall. A dome made a bulge beyond the eave.

Jefferies halted the Rover near the site and climbed out, with Merrin and Francis following. Merrin's heart was pounding, and his fingers itched to touch the ancient wall, learn its secrets, uncover its past. Francis appeared to be even more eager, rushing past Merrin and shooting half a dozen paces ahead. Merrin loudly and pointedly cleared his throat. Francis stopped and cast a guilty look over his shoulder. A blush crawled over his face, and he gave a tentative, sheepish grin.

"Sorry!" he said. "I get the fever too, you know. Your dig. You first."

Merrin relented and trotted forward to join him. "Let's have a look, then. Jefferies, get some of the men to unload the new supplies. Then I'll need you and Chuma to show me around."

"Right," Jefferies said, and left.

Merrin led Francis toward the structure. A trench had been dug beside the wall, putting the eave at head level for anyone standing at the bottom. A small team of native workers dressed in khaki shirts were digging around the perimeter with trowels and small shovels, but none of them were very sweaty, and Merrin suspected that with both their manager and their foreman away from the site, the workers had done more resting than digging. He was also glad to see that they were at least dumping the dirt into wooden wheelbarrows so it could be sifted later for bits of pottery, bones, broken tools, and other missed relics.

About twenty-five or thirty feet of the wall had been uncovered from side to side, and the trench just barely reached the corner of the building. Deciding to plunge right in, Merrin jumped down into the trench, pulled a wide brush from his pocket, and began removing the fine layer of dust that had settled on the wall since its excavation. The wall was built of stone blocks, perfectly shaped and mortared.

"It reminds me of Roman architecture," Francis said from the top of the trench. "But more exotic."

"Is this your first assignment, Father?" Merrin asked without looking up.

"Yes. Before this, I was studying at the Archives in the Holy See."

"The Vatican itself. Impressive." A dirty cloud surrounded Merrin. "But not exactly training for missionary work."

Francis shifted uncomfortably, then asked, "What do you think of the building?"

Merrin continued brushing dust. The wall beneath was white. "I would guess fourth or fifth century," he said. "And it's definitely Byzantine, not Roman. Look at those designs on the cornice at the corner. They look like stylized trees with people standing among the bushes beneath them. Byzantine."

"I'll take your word for it," Francis said. "The Byzantine era is a bit outside my area of expertise."

The admission somehow mollified Merrin, and he thawed. A little. "You may as well come down, Father. I can't talk when you're up there."

Francis dropped into the trench, lightly and without hesitation. It was cooler down here out of the sunlight. Sand and gravel crunched under his boots. "This is going to be a big job," he said. "You must feel like a mosquito in a nudist colony."

Merrin blinked at him. "What?"

"So much to do, you don't know where to start."

There was a moment of silence. Then both men burst out laughing. Merrin felt himself thaw further yet.

After the laughing stopped, Merrin took off his hat, wiped his sweaty forehead on his sleeve, and gestured at the stonework.

"The craftsmanship is amazing," he said. "Each block perfectly carved and smoothed. You can't even see the chisel marks."

"It's beautiful," Francis agreed, though he began to sound puzzled. "Forgive my ignorance, but should the stones look so new?"

"What?"

"The stones." Francis pointed. "They're shiny where you've brushed the dust away. Like they're brand-new."

"That's not . . . not possible." Merrin brushed some more, working his way toward the corner. Francis was right—the stones were slick and shiny under their layer of dust. "These stones are centuries old. They should be severely weathered. It's almost as if . . . as if . . ."

"As if what?" Francis said.

Merrin ignored him. "Chuma!" he shouted. "Chuma! I need a bigger brush!"

Chuma's big form appeared at the top of the trench. "Yes, Mr. Merrin!"

A moment later, the foreman handed one down to Merrin, who set to cleaning dust and dirt from the corner of the buried church. Again Francis asked what was wrong, but Merrin didn't seem to hear. More of the edge came to light under Merrin's swift, sure strokes, and the corner showed up sharp and precise. After a long moment, Merrin leaned back against the wall of the trench behind him, a stunned look on his face.

"Impossible," he breathed.

Above, Chuma said something in Turkana that Will didn't catch. He looked up and saw the same look of stunned amazement on the foreman's face.

"I still don't understand," Francis said, clearly starting to get a little angry about it.

Merrin seemed to shake off the trance he was in. "Look closer at the blocks, Francis. What do you see?"

He looked. "I see a wonderful example of fine-cut masonry, probably done in the fourth or fifth century, like you said. Beautifully preserved, too."

"It seems almost new, doesn't it?" Merrin said. "Virtually no erosion."

Light dawned on Francis's face. "But the wind and sun up here—it should be badly weathered."

"And damaged," Merrin said. "I was operating on the assumption that this structure had been buried as the result of a landslide or earthquake, but we should have seen some damage to the walls by now."

"It looks pristine to me," Francis said. "Perfectly new."

"Exactly," Merrin said. "Either someone in this century built a church using fifth-century building methods and materials—something I sincerely doubt—or this building was deliberately buried. Right after it was built."

"They came here and built something only to *bury* it? That doesn't make sense."

"Not with this kind of structure, no. Countless cultures build things to bury—the Egyptians are the most famous example—but the Byzantine Empire never bought into the idea."

"Not that anyone knows of, anyway," Chuma said from above. "Perhaps these Byzantines buried dozens of churches and this is the first one anyone has found, eh?"

"Again, possible," Merrin concluded, "but it doesn't seem likely, especially since we're so far south of the old Byzantine Empire."

"Maybe it's a tomb," Francis guessed, getting into the spirit of the discussion.

"Well, we won't know until we have a better look," Merrin said, and rubbed his hands together in a brisk movement. "Chuma, prepare the men to work double shifts. I want these walls cleared, and I want to go inside."

The blood of the bull lay red and sticky on Jomo's hands. He would not wash them or his machete until sunset, for the blood of the sacrifice would grant him both power and protection. He feared that he and the rest of the village would need a great deal of both. The first white man made Jomo uneasy, though he had made no attempt to convert Jomo's people to the cult of his tortured god. The second white man was another matter entirely. Unlike the first one, the second wore the black-and-white collar, and Jomo assumed that meant he was more likely to preach.

Jomo leaned on his blood-tipped spear and looked down at the site. Some of his own relatives were working for the whites, digging and brushing. This work made Jomo uneasy, and the strange building made him shudder. It was only blocks of stone, but it made him think of a jackal hiding in a thicket, waiting to leap out with strong teeth and ghoulish laughter.

Chuma, who had been kneeling at the edge of the trench, abruptly straightened and boomed orders at the workers waiting nearby. They sprang into action like termites on a mound. Jomo wanted to run down and tell them to stop, to leave this place alone. But he didn't. Instead, he stood and watched and leaned on his spear, trying to quell the unreasoning fear that grew like a cold vine around his heart.

Four

✠

Archaeological survey site, British East Africa

Regular work tires a woman but totally wrecks a man.

—Kenyan proverb

IT WAS LATE AFTERNOON, three days later. The native men were clearing the walls of the church all the way around, working with the sort of enthusiasm only a wage increase can bring. Appalled at how little Jefferies had been paying the workers, Merrin had ordered an immediate raise, much to Jefferies's obvious chagrin. Merrin wondered if the man had been skimming and made a mental note to take a close look at the books when he had a chance. At the moment, however, there was simply too much to do.

He had risen from his bed back at the hotel long before sunrise and been on-site before the sky reached full brightness, brushing, measuring, examining, exploring. It hadn't taken long for the old rhythms to come back to him, and he found himself issuing orders to Chuma and the men with the ease and confidence of long practice. He used Father Francis as a sort of assistant, making him oversee the sifting of debris, ensuring the workers had water, taking notes, and keeping track of the dozens of other little tasks that could bog a chief archaeologist down. Merrin had to admit he took a little perverse pleasure in handing the scut work off to the young priest.

The church was proving surprisingly easy to uncover. The soil was loose and sandy, almost falling away beneath the workmen's small shovels and trowels. It was a miracle the building had stayed buried as long as it had. The trench now surrounded the entire structure, and in some places was a full two meters deep and two meters wide. Like all Christian cathedrals, the building was in the shape of a cross that pointed east. The long arm of the cross, called the main aisle, was exactly twenty-two and a half meters wide and thirty-three meters long. The north-south transepts—the short arms of the cross—were ten meters wide, not counting the domed nave, where the short and long arms crossed.

The dome tempted Merrin. This church was a puzzle to beat all puzzles, and the answers lay inside. It was pushing archaeological standards to enter through the dome so early in the dig, but Merrin was feeling the stirrings of a new go-to-hell attitude.

Merrin tried to get a solid grip on the top of the trench where he had been photographing sections of the outer wall and heave himself out of the trench, but he couldn't. He slipped, went back to the bottom in a shower of sandy soil, tried again. This time a large, strong hand grabbed his wrist and helped haul him up.

"You need a ladder," Chuma said, brushing Merrin down once he had his feet. "Perhaps we should dig a ramp."

"Good idea," Merrin said. "Where's Jefferies? I want to go inside the—"

A laughing scream slashed the air. Merrin jumped and tried to look in all directions at once. He saw nothing but beshrubbed, rocky hills. Another laugh echoed, closer this time, and the cold sound curdled Merrin's blood.

"Hyenas?" he said nervously.

Chuma, unperturbed, nodded. "They've been a constant menace since we broke ground."

"Even during the day?"

"Yes. Mutib—he is my cousin and a fine hunter, you know—Mutib says he has seen more and more hyenas about in the last two months. Mutib likes to tell stories—his favorite is one in which he outraced a tiger—but in this I believe him."

Not far away from the two men, a worker dropped the basket of soil he was carrying. The dirt spilled out and the man fell writhing to the dusty ground. Merrin and Chuma traded a startled glance, then rushed over to help. The worker's eyes rolled back in his head and convulsions shook his body. Incoherent words tumbled in a torrent from his mouth as he twisted and flopped like a beached fish. When Merrin's shadow fell across him, he screamed in terror. He tried to back away from the looming figure, but his muscles still sent him into twisting fits.

"*Wai ekipe nikiar!*" he cried. "*Ekipe wai kimiekinae!*"

"He thinks you are a devil," Chuma said, kneeling next to the man. "He is asking you to spare him."

Merrin leaned down and put a hand on the man's forehead. It was hot and dry. "I'm not a devil, friend," he said soothingly. "It's all right."

Chuma translated the words, but the worker twisted anyway. He tried to rise, but his body betrayed him and he fell back to the dust with a grunt of pain. Securing a stable hold on the worker, Chuma gently and firmly cradled the man's head on his own arm. A crowd of onlookers was already assembling. Chuma spoke quiet words in Turkana, and Merrin assumed they were of reassurance. Will Francis arrived, looking worried.

"Send for the doctor," Merrin told him. "This man is hallucinating."

"I already did," Francis replied. "She's on-site today because of that worker who sprained his ankle this morning."

"What's wrong with him?" Merrin asked.

"The heat," Chuma said, sending a hard look in Merrin's direction. "We have driven the men too hard."

Merrin rubbed his chin. He had suspected heat sickness as well, but he had never seen it accompanied by convulsions and hallucinations. But then, he admitted to himself, he wasn't a doctor.

Chuma gestured to two workers and said, "*Todauk kiwapakinae.*" The men obeyed, picking up the stricken man and following Merrin down toward the tents pitched near the dig. A series of worktables had been set up there, shaded beneath canvas shelters. Merrin ducked into one of the tents, snagged a cup and a water bag, and emerged in time to see Chuma and the two workmen set the man down in the shade near one of the tables. Merrin filled the cup with water and passed it to Chuma, who pressed it to the man's lips. He resisted at first, then began to drink, slurping the water down in great gulps.

"Don't let him take too much at once," Merrin cautioned.

"I know," Chuma said, pulling the cup away. "I have dealt with heat sickness before."

Merrin removed his hat, wiped sweat from his forehead, and glanced around the site. Men continued to work diligently under the blazing sun, trowels, shovels, and brushes in continuous motion. Everything smelled of hot dust and dry dirt. Grit got into everything, making Merrin's skin itch and drying out his eyes. It was a familiar feeling on a dig, though he didn't remember the sun getting this hot before. Was it warmer than usual, or was he just getting older?

"We should break off in the afternoons," he suggested. "Resume in the evenings."

"Or work shorter hours," Chuma said, the rebuke clear in his voice.

Sarah emerged from one of the tents with a black bag and trotted over. Straw-blond hair made becomingly curly in the heat poked out from under her hat, and Merrin was seized with an urge to give one lock a gentle tug, like a schoolboy seeking attention.

"What's wrong with him?" Sarah asked, kneeling next to the man and taking a stethoscope out of her bag.

Chuma explained as she examined the man. Merrin's gaze, meanwhile, drifted over to a group of workers standing a short distance away. They stared at him with stony faces, outrage written in their posture. They looked ready to tear him apart. Merrin wanted to look away and found he couldn't. He remembered stories of wild beasts who wouldn't attack until you broke eye contact, and he knew in that moment they were thinking the exact same thing. Would they rush him?

Cold fear trickled down Merrin's back, and he involuntarily backed up a step. His foot came down on Chuma's instep, causing Merrin to stumble and look away. The motion broke the spell, and Merrin suddenly felt foolish. The workers muttered among themselves but didn't rush forward like the howling savages of his silly imagination.

"They blame the British," Chuma said.

"For what?" Merrin asked.

"For uncovering the church. They believe it's cursed."

Merrin automatically glanced over at the building. A four-legged animal was standing on the dome. Merrin squinted into the bright sun. A hyena? He blinked, and the animal was gone. Merrin shook his head. Now *he* was seeing things.

"Maybe I should take a little walk," Merrin said. "Give the men a break from . . . from . . . well, just to give the men a break."

Before Chuma could respond, Merrin strode away from the collapsed worker and the hateful gazes of the other men. He went down into a shallow canyon a ways from the site, trying to figure out what was going on at this dig. The canyon walls offered a little relief from the overbearing sun and gave him the feeling that he was indoors.

Merrin took a drink of warm water from the canteen hooked to his belt. He still had no clue about who Semelier was or why he thought a Sumerian artifact would be found in a Byzantine church buried in East Africa. He didn't know why the church had been built, or why it had been buried. He couldn't understand why the place made the natives so nervous. He needed more information, and he supposed the only way to get it was to keep digging.

Gravel rustled above Merrin's head and a handful of stones clattered onto the canyon floor. A pang shot through Merrin, and he thought of giggling hyenas. He looked up and just caught sight of a boy disappearing around an outcropping. The boy looked familiar.

"Joseph?" Merrin called. He trotted forward. More gravel skittered down the canyon wall. "Joseph!" This time his tone was more anxious.

A shadow fell on the ground behind him and glided closer. Merrin saw it out of the corner of his eye. He spun around. No one there. He looked up. Joseph was perched on a rock halfway up the canyon wall. The boy gave a cheery wave.

"*Harabi*, Mr. Merrin!" he called, and jumped down to the ground with a youthful agility Merrin could only remember. Merrin shook his head.

"Are you out here by yourself?" he said.

Joseph nodded. "I'm collecting rocks." He gestured at his trouser pockets. They bulged with uneven lumps.

"That's quite a treasure," Merrin said, amused. "Careful your trousers don't fall off."

"I have suspenders," Joseph said, clearly proud of his cleverness. "See?" He snapped one of them.

Merrin smiled. Nice kid. He opened one of the kit bags attached to his belt and pulled out a small hammer. Instead of a claw opposite the head, this hammer had a little spike. The whole thing weighed barely a pound and was meant for delicate work.

"Since you're clearly dedicated and well prepared as a rock hound," Merrin said, "I believe you're about ready for one of these. It's a real rock hammer, like professional diggers use."

He handed the tool to Joseph, who looked at it with pleased amazement. "Thank you, Mr. Merrin! I will use it every day."

"You're welcome," Merrin said, and turned to go.

"I know a secret."

The tone of the boy's voice, high-pitched and strange, made Merrin stop. "Really? What is it?"

Joseph leaned forward and whispered, "I know why Father Francis is really here."

What on earth? Merrin thought. "Why is he here, Joseph?"

"To save our souls." He flashed Merrin a grin and ran off toward the dig site. Merrin shrugged and followed. This was no secret—in addition to his work at the site, Will Francis was setting up a school in an unused room back at Emekwi's hotel, and priest-run schools made no bones about the true purpose behind the reading, writing, and Latin.

Back at the site, Merrin saw things had calmed down. The workers were digging again, though at a slower pace, while Chuma and Jefferies supervised. The only person who noticed Merrin had returned was Sarah. She was standing outside the tent set aside as an on-site clinic, watching the downed worker being helped away by a pair of friends. Merrin headed over, intending to ask about the man.

Is that the only reason you want to see her? whispered that inner voice. *Careful you don't break any of those vows.*

"Shut up," he muttered.

"Pardon?" Sarah asked. She was closer than he had thought.

"Nothing," Merrin said quickly. "Just talking to myself. How's our man?"

"His seizures stopped." The doctor had removed her hat, and she had to shade her eyes against the sun's glare. "I wanted to keep him at the hospital for observation, but he wouldn't stay. I think the Turkana have stopped trusting my medicine."

"That must make your job difficult," Merrin said.

"You have no idea." She ducked back into the medical tent and Merrin followed. The tent's interior was almost as hot as the exterior. Dim light filtered through the canvas, and Merrin smelled disinfectant. Sarah went over to a water bucket, rolled up her sleeves, and scrubbed her hands. A string of blue numbers marched across her inner forearm. Merrin stared at them, then looked away. Sarah noticed. She turned her back, dried her hands, and jerked her sleeves back down.

"Water?" she said.

"Yes, thank you," Merrin said, glad of something to break the silence.

She poured him a cupful from a container made from a large gourd and handed it to him. The water was tepid, and Merrin wondered what it would be like to drink something cold again.

"So what is it you hope to find here?" Sarah asked, pouring herself some water and sitting neatly on a camp stool.

Merrin finished the water. "The answer to how a church ended up in this place a thousand years before Christianity arrived."

The doctor looked him up and down, and Merrin felt oddly naked. "You *were* a priest once, weren't you?"

The question surprised him. "Yes."

"What happened?"

Merrin looked into Sarah's blue eyes. They weren't hard or harsh as he had been expecting. Instead he saw genuine compassion there, something he hadn't seen in a long, long time. Something inside him shifted a tiny bit, and a crack appeared in a wall he had thrown up long ago. The tattoo marked Sarah as a survivor, just as he was. She, of all people, might understand where the Church had not.

"It was just before the War ended, and there was a shortage of priests," he said. "So I was pulled away from field archaeology and put in charge of a parish in a village called Hellendoorn in Holland."

"Holland was occupied by the Nazis," Sarah said quietly.

Merrin nodded. "The previous priest had . . . disappeared, and I was his replacement." He paused and cleared his throat. "One day, a Nazi soldier found—"

"Bloody savages!" The tent flap was ripped aside and Jefferies stormed inside. His face was faintly sunburned, and his boils looked a little better. "Stupid fuzzies can't wipe their own arses without instruction."

The man's entrance destroyed the moment. Sarah strode for the exit. "I have to get back to town."

Merrin opened his mouth to say something, but Jefferies beat him to it. "Wait!"

Sarah's hand was on the tent flap, but she stopped and reluctantly turned to face him. Jefferies shuffled his feet uncomfortably and looked shy. Merrin grimaced. On a boy's face the expression would have been cute. On Jefferies's pocked face, it looked inhuman.

"I found this," Jefferies said, and held up a round medal, tarnished with age. On it was an image of a bearded man holding a child. Both man and child had halos. The medal hung on a new chain. "It's St. Joseph. For luck."

He moved forward, obviously intending to put it on her, but she shied away.

"Please," Jefferies said. "For my behavior."

After a moment, Sarah nodded and turned her back so Jefferies could put the chain around her neck. She kept her eyes, however, on Merrin. Jefferies noticed.

"What the hell are you doing?" he snarled.

For a moment, Merrin thought Jefferies was talking

73

to him. Then he saw Joseph standing in the doorway of the tent looking like a gazelle cornered by a lion.

"Get the fuck out of here, you little scab!" Jefferies snatched up a heavy alcohol bottle and started to throw. Merrin sprang forward and caught his wrist.

"Don't!" Merrin snapped.

Sarah, meanwhile, spirited Joseph out of the tent and away. Merrin stood there, eyes locked with Jefferies's. He could feel the other man strain against his grip, but Merrin was the stronger. After a moment, Jefferies relaxed. Merrin let go and took the bottle away.

"Yeah, all right," Jefferies muttered. "Didn't realize you were a fuzzy lover, Merrin. Buggers get into everything—"

"How long," Merrin interrupted, "will it take you to get the doors to the church uncovered?"

Jefferies furrowed his brow, bringing a set of boils into a single, temporary lump. "A few days."

"And how do we get inside in the meantime?"

"*We* don't," Jefferies said. "Chuma'll take you in through the roof."

Five

✠

Archaeological survey site, British East Africa

No one knows caution as a regret.
> —Kenyan proverb

LANKESTER MERRIN CLUNG to the rope and slid down through darkness. Above him, the open dome gaped like a mouth, revealing warm blue sky. Below was a large circle of light that encompassed a smaller speck of light. The speck jumped and bobbed nervously. Merrin clenched his gloved hands to control his slide as he drew closer to the bottom. At the right moment, he jumped clear of the rope and landed on a hard stone floor.

Chuma was waiting for him, noticeably uneasy. The opening in the dome dropped a circle of dusty white light on the floor, and the foreman remained in its exact center, holding a lit lantern. Merrin tried to see beyond the gloom into the church, but the light prevented him from seeing into the darkness.

The interior was cool and smelled of dust. Merrin had half expected it to be damp, but of course the air was perfectly dry in this desert climate. He got the sense of a great open space around him.

A shadow fell across him. Chuma jumped and Merrin dodged aside like a startled lion, but it was only William Francis descending on the same rope. He dropped to the floor with a lithe grace that Merrin remembered from his younger days. His khaki shirt was open, displaying his Roman collar.

"Following us, Father?" Merrin asked, his voice bouncing and echoing around them. "Or playing the part of Church representative?"

Francis ignored the question. He stared about instead, trying to pierce the inky blackness that surrounded them. "Is it safe to walk around?"

The answer, of course, was an emphatic no. Any number of things could be waiting in the darkness—rubble, weakened or collapsed flooring, even animals who had found their way in through cracks and crevices. They should establish a safe perimeter and bring down more powerful lighting equipment, then do an engineering survey to see if the structure appeared sound. But Merrin was abruptly annoyed with Francis's presence again, and his earlier go-to-hell feeling plucked at him.

"Let's find out," he said, and picked up a second lantern Chuma had set on the floor. He lit it and took a deep breath. No human had set foot in this church for probably a thousand years, and he was going to be the first to explore it. For an irrational moment he recalled the folklore of his childhood, that the first person to enter a house on New Year's Day should be a dark-haired man. Merrin was fair-haired, which meant bad luck. On the other hand, Chuma had actually entered first, and he had dark hair. Merrin shook his head. Foolishness. He pushed the idea aside and left the circle of light. Francis and Chuma came right behind him.

Twice in his career thus far Merrin had entered places that no human had trod for countless ages. Each time it seemed like there should be some kind of strange feeling, a tingle or a rush of wind. It never happened. It didn't this time, either. Merrin stepped into the darkness, his lantern light sweeping the area ahead of him.

As a precaution, Merrin checked the floor first. It was smooth and flat, the same worked stone as the outside walls. Space echoed around him, and he could sense the height of the ceiling far overhead. No pews, of course—ancient churches expected the congregation to stand throughout the service. Though what kind of service would have been conducted all the way out here?

Ahead of him, the main aisle stretched into a blackness that swallowed his lantern beam. Two parallel rows of columns reached up to the ceiling, dividing the main aisle into thirds and creating galleries that ran up the left and right sides of the aisle. Merrin nodded. Normal cathedral construction so far. The ceiling was high, but not as high as those allowed by the new construction techniques perfected at the Santiago de Compostela cathedral in eleventh-century Spain. No windows, either, not even the thin, narrow ones this sort of structure could support. That only reinforced the idea that this church had been built with the intention of burying it. Merrin stared around in awe. An exultation filled him. He was looking at a lifetime of study right here. So much to learn, so much to find out. Ancient secrets lay hidden in this church, and Merrin would be the one who ferreted them out.

Dust lay thick on the floor, and the motes stirred by Merrin's footsteps danced in the light of his lantern. He heard Francis and Chuma behind him, silent except for their breathing. He wondered if they were thinking the same thing he was.

They were almost all the way to the main entrance when Francis's lantern jiggled drunkenly as he tried to open his canteen one-handed. Even in a place of awe, Merrin reflected, the physical needs still held sway. He looked more closely at the huge columns. They were dusty white and massive as trees.

"This is very strange," he mused with a thoughtful expression.

"Stranger than a Byzantine church in the middle of an African desert?" Francis said. "What do you mean?"

"This place has no windows, and those doors at the end don't look like they were meant to open easily," Merrin replied. "You aren't meant to get in and out of this place."

"Including us," Chuma put in morosely.

A deep, hollow hiss echoed almost beneath their feet. Francis made an incoherent sound and leaped back. The canteen thumped unheeded to the floor. Something slithered across the floor and away. Chuma's light picked out a thick, serpentine body the color of sand.

"Puff adder," he said. "Very deadly. My nephew's best friend was bitten by one, and it took him two days to die. A good thing you did not step on it, Father."

"Thank God," Francis exhaled with fervor. "How did it get in here?"

"Cracks and crevices underground," Merrin said. "I've seen it before." He played his light across the walls. They were lined with mosaics, thousands upon thousands of shiny tiles that made up pictures. Merrin's eye automatically went to the mosaic closest to the entrance and he backtracked to the doors so he could examine it more closely. Through the space between the first two columns he saw a picture of an empty throne—God's, presumably—surrounded by angels. One angel, blond, was taller and more beautiful than the others. Beyond the second archway, Lucifer was gathering his hosts. In the third, he and his allies rose up against Michael and the other angels. The war continued for three more mosaics. Then Michael's angels flung Lucifer and those who fought for him out of heaven. They fell, and as they fell, their beautiful faces and fine bodies twisted and tore. By the time they landed in hell, they had become gibbering demons. In the final mosaic, a defiant Lucifer ruled below, while a triumphant Michael exulted above.

"Lucifer," Francis breathed beside Merrin. "God's favorite angel. Cast out after the war in heaven. Astounding."

"Not bad," Merrin said, suddenly unwilling to be awed by anything that impressed Francis, though he did find the mosaics rather unusual. "It's more customary to show the fourteen Stations of the Cross, not the war in heaven."

They had come back to the nave again. To the left and the right were two smaller chambers that made up the short arms of the cross-shaped building. They stayed outside of the lit area to avoid ruining their night vision, but the darkness was heavy and oppressive. The twisted demons on the mosaics seemed to be reaching out of the walls, scratching the air with their claws and biting at it with their teeth, hungry for something real to feed upon.

Something flashed past Merrin's head in a flutter of wings. He almost dove for cover, then caught himself and simply ducked, heart pounding at the back of his throat. Francis yelped and Chuma let out a barking cry and waved his hat around. Coarse caws filled the air, spinning and echoing through the church. Something scratched the back of Merrin's neck with a white line of pain. Warm blood trickled into his collar.

"Crows!" Merrin shouted, clapping his hand to the back of his neck. The flock vanished into the dark church, though Merrin could still hear their eerie croaks and caws.

Chuma shone his lantern in the direction of the noise and let out a low whistle. At the end of the church beyond the nave was a group of four white statues on pedestals. All four statues sported wings and robes. They faced each other around an enormous block of stone topped by an altar of rectangular stone, at which the statues were pointing weapons—a flaming sword, a normal sword, a spear, and a mace. The crows had gathered on one of the stone figures, muttering and croaking among themselves like old women dressed in black rags. More mosaics glittered on the altar and its dais.

"Who are they?" Chuma asked.

"The one with the spear is probably Gabriel," Francis said in a teacher voice. "The one with the flaming sword is Uriel. The fourth one is likely Raphael, though he usually carries a staff and not a mace. The one the crows are sitting on is Archangel Michael."

"Actually, they're all Archangel Michael," Merrin said.

"What?" Francis asked. "How could you know that?"

"The base of each one has the word 'Michael' inscribed on it in Greek."

Francis shone his light downward. His face fell. "Oh. Archangel Michael."

"The right hand of God," Merrin added, unable to keep a malicious tone from his voice.

The crows shifted and muttered, glaring down at the men with glittering yellow eyes. A splat hit the floor beneath the statue, and Merrin smelled bird shit. He moved cautiously forward, his light spreading through the darkness around the altar. He climbed the three steps up to the top of the dais. A feeling of unease stole over him, and he realized all the angels' weapons were pointed directly at him. Or rather, they were pointed at the altar on the dais. There was barely room to move without bumping into something pointed, confirming Merrin's theory that this church wasn't meant to be used for worship—no priest could use this altar without skewering himself.

"The crows must have flown in through the dome," Chuma said. "Have you ever seen anything like this church?"

"Not this far from Rome," Merrin said.

"What's the reason for multiple Michaels?" Francis asked, still sounding wounded that Merrin had punctured his earlier deduction.

"No idea," Merrin admitted, rubbing his raspy chin. "Michael is God's warrior. Maybe the builders thought they needed an army."

"Very strange," Francis muttered. He moved up to join Merrin on the dais. "It doesn't look like any church I've ever seen. Churches are built to exalt heaven, but this—all their weapons are pointed downward. As if . . ."

He trailed off. One of the crows scratched its head with quick fluttering movements of its claws. Merrin moved around to the other side of the altar, and his lantern beam picked out a broken beam of wood jutting up behind it like a shattered finger. He ducked under a stony mace and looked closer. It appeared to be the base to something. The jagged part of the wood looked newer, as if it had been recently broken. Merrin's eyebrows drew together.

"Francis, come look at this," he said, and Francis joined him.

"Strange," Francis said. "What could—"

A giant face loomed in the darkness. Merrin jumped. "Francis! Behind you!"

Francis spun and snapped his light around. The face was upside down. Mouth open in a silent wail, eyes dead and hollow beneath a crown of thorns, it wept in silent agony. Francis shrank back, then realized the face was carved of wood. He ran his light farther upward, revealing a huge crucifix—Christ on the cross. A massive chain was wrapped around its feet, suspending it head down from the ceiling. The broken base was an exact match to the top of the jagged beam. The crucifix was half again life-size.

"Lord, have mercy on us," Francis whispered. "Why would someone do this?"

"A more important question is *who* would do this," Merrin said, "and *how*. No one's been in this place for a thousand years." He reached out and touched the figure's face.

The crows exploded from their perch. They rushed through the air, moaning and croaking. Their wings beat against Merrin's head and shoulders, and he threw up his hands to protect his face. Hot pain sliced his ear. He screamed and lashed out with his fist. It connected with something feathery that crunched. Air swirled around Merrin, beaten by harsh black wings. Another crow nipped at his wrist, drawing yet more blood. Chuma was shouting something—

—and then the crows were gone. Merrin looked up in time to see the last of the flock vanish out of the dome. He sucked at his wrist, then gingerly touched his ear. The crow had taken a fair piece out of the top, and it was bleeding in a small waterfall. It felt as if it had been torn halfway off.

"You mates all right down there?" Jefferies called from above. "Those bloody birds looked pretty nasty going in and out."

"We should go back up," Francis insisted to Merrin. "You need to see Dr. Novack."

"Get ready to take Mr. Merrin up!" Chuma called. "He has minor injuries."

"Right, then!"

The rope was part of a block and tackle set up on the church roof. In short order, Jefferies hauled Merrin, then Francis, and then Chuma out of the interior. Merrin flinched at the bright daylight until his eyes readjusted.

"They got you a good one, mate," Jefferies said, noticing Merrin's ear. "Christ!"

"There's no need to blaspheme," Francis said primly.

"Head wounds always bleed a lot," Merrin assured them, taking out his handkerchief and pressing it to his ear. The entire shoulder of his shirt was soaked in scarlet. "I've had much worse."

Jefferies shrugged. "So what did you find?"

"A puzzle." Merrin fixed Jefferies with a hard stare. "Mr. Jefferies, I think there's something you haven't told me."

"Eh? What do you mean?"

"I mean that it's clear *someone* has been inside this church, and recently."

"I have no idea what you're talking about, mate," he said, but his hand stole upward to finger one of the boils on his face.

"The base of that crucifix was broken within the last month or two. Someone's been in there. What aren't you telling me, Mr. Jefferies?"

The dig manager returned Merrin's hard stare for a

moment, then looked away, still fingering the boil. "I suppose there's no harm in talking about it now."

"Not if you want to keep your job, there isn't," Merrin agreed.

"Look, mate—I'm only doing what Bession told me."

"Who's Bession?" Francis asked.

"He was the chief archaeologist before you lot arrived," Jefferies said, "and the one what uncovered the dome here. He saw it could be opened, and he wanted to have a little peek inside, you know? But he didn't want anyone to find out."

"Because that would be poor archaeology, and he would be castigated for it by our little community," Merrin asserted, suddenly and uncomfortably aware of his own desire for haste. "Go on."

"So the two of us came out here one night and got the thing open, yeah? That was a weird night. Windy and such, and when we pulled up the dome, it . . . breathed on us. Almost made me wet my nappies, if you know what I'm sayin'. Bession went down for a few hours, then I helped him back up. He asked if I wanted to have a look, but you couldn't pay me enough to go down there, so I stayed up here, thank you very much. Bession went down there two more times, always at night. Swore me to secrecy about the whole thing. I thought it was a little strange, but I figured, hey, Bession's a frog, and the Frenchies are always a bit strange. Bugger anything that moves, they will, including the boys. 'Course, I always say live and let live, but even I can't—"

"The *point*, Mr. Jefferies," Merrin interrupted.

"Right. Anyway, he went down there a few times and I helped him. That's the long and short of it."

"Is there an inventory of what Bession found down there?"

Jefferies shrugged. "I never saw one."

"Chuma, did you know about this?"

"I did not," Chuma said promptly, and Merrin believed him.

"Where is this Bession?" Merrin demanded. "I need to talk to him."

"You can't," Chuma said.

Merrin raised an eyebrow. "Why not?"

"He's gone mad."

"Mad?" Francis echoed.

At this Jefferies nodded. "Starkers. Right round the bend, he went."

"Where are his notes, then?" Merrin said, sounding more frustrated with every word.

"In his tent." Chuma pointed. "It is over there."

Bession's battered tent whipped in the wind. The sides belled and collapsed, then belled again. It was a large tent, the size of a truck. Merrin, glad his ear had finally stopped bleeding, reached for the ties. Francis and Jefferies he had sent to do other work. Francis went with bad grace, Jefferies with alacrity.

"No one's been inside since Bession fell ill?" Merrin asked.

"They are superstitious," Chuma said.

"And you?"

"Not superstitious." He tapped his forehead. "Smart."

Releasing the final tie, Merrin opened the flap and stepped inside. The tent's interior was a total mess, as if a set of filing cabinets had exploded. Camp tables and chairs were scattered everywhere, and most surfaces were covered with papers. A cot with a rumpled blanket thrown carelessly across it occupied one corner while a messy desk occupied another. Merrin was rather startled. Some archaeologists were less than meticulous about their surroundings, but this seemed a bit extreme.

He went over to the desk and felt a little jerk in his stomach. Glaring up from the papers were drawings of demons. Dozens of demons. Demons with horns. Demons with tentacles. Demons with slime dripping from their pores. Demons raping women. Demons sodomizing men. Demons devouring children. Demons drinking blood. And in the center of them all was the demon from Semelier's rubbing.

Merrin's injured ear throbbed. He reached down to pick up the latter drawing. The moment he touched it, pain lanced his finger and he snatched his hand back. Blood oozed from a cut on the pad of his index finger and dropped red onto Semelier's demon. Merrin grimaced—this was his fourth injury today. More carefully this time, he lifted the drawing. Beneath it lay a shard of broken glass.

"Chuma, where is—" he began, and then realized the foreman had not followed him into the tent. He raised his voice. "Chuma!"

Chuma stuck his head inside. "Yes?" He saw the mess and grimaced. "You are not asking me to clean this up, are you?"

"No. Where is Bession now?"

"The sanitarium in Nairobi."

"I'll have to visit him," Merrin said. "He has a lot to . . . to . . ." The words died away as something else caught his eye. Slowly, unwillingly, his gaze went up to the roof of the tent. Chuma craned his neck to see what Merrin was staring at, and his mouth dropped open. Large red-brown symbols covered the ceiling. The wind rippled the canvas, making the symbols writhe around the roof's underside like a nest of snakes.

Unease stole over Merrin. "How long has Bession been gone?" he asked.

"A few weeks," answered the foreman, visibly shaken. "I brought him to Nairobi, and then Major Granville told me you were coming, so I waited for you."

Merrin frowned. "Is Bession an expert in biblical languages?"

"I don't know," Chuma said. His voice was hushed. "Why?"

"Because this writing is Aramaic, the language spoken in Palestine at the time of Christ."

Fear slid across Chuma's face. "What . . . what does it say?"

" 'The Fallen shall rise in a river of blood.' "

The last of the sunlight vanished from the sky, leaving behind a black sky salted with jewel-bright stars. Merrin parked the jeep in front of Derati's little hospital and killed both engine and headlights. The village looked nearly deserted. Few lights brightened any windows. A lonely wind rushed up the street, making the trees beyond the village dance and hiss in the darkness. The road and boardwalks were empty. Merrin climbed down from the jeep and headed for the hospital door. Tinny music floated out to greet him. He poked his head inside.

The main room of the hospital contained a row of neatly made beds, each with a tray table sitting next to it. None of the beds were occupied. Wooden cabinets and shelves of medical equipment lined the walls. The place smelled of ether and rubbing alcohol. Merrin saw no one. He thought a moment, then went around to the back of the building. Sarah had to live somewhere, and Merrin guessed her quarters were attached.

Around back, he found a low porch with a screen door. Light spilled out onto the boards. Merrin approached the door and peered into a small, spare kitchen. A tiny wood stove occupied one corner, a washbasin the other. Wooden crates nailed high on the walls made shelves for pots, dishes, and food. A pair of hanging kerosene lamps provided warm yellow light.

Sarah sat at the tiny table with her back to Merrin, holding a pack of cards. Three cards lay faceup on the table in front of her, and Merrin could see them over her shoulder. The first showed a tower being struck by lightning. The second showed an armored skeleton riding a white horse. The third showed a horned, winged devil looming over the naked, chained figures of a man and woman.

Merrin knew he should knock or speak to alert her to his presence, but he stayed silent. He found he liked watching her. Sarah, meanwhile, put the three cards back into the deck, shuffled, and dealt three more cards.

They were exactly the same, right down to the order they came up. Odd. Sarah stared down at the bits of pasteboard, and Merrin felt abruptly like a voyeur. He knocked. Sarah started and twisted around in her chair.

"Hello," Merrin said cheerfully. "Do you have a moment?"

Sarah recovered herself and smiled. "Of course. Come in."

Merrin carefully wiped his feet on the mat and opened the door to enter.

"Can I get you some tea?" Sarah said, rising. "Or something more substantial?"

"Thank you," Merrin said, letting the door swing shut behind him. "That would be—"

"Good God!" Sarah exclaimed. "What happened to your ear? And your shirt—it's covered with blood!"

"I had a little accident," Merrin admitted. "Can you . . . ?"

"Of course! Please sit down. I'll be right back." She vanished into the clinic.

Merrin sat in the chair Sarah had vacated. It was warm from her body, and it felt oddly intimate, sharing her heat this way. The faceup tarot cards and the pack lay on the table in front of him. The Church frowned heavily on the occult, even something as minor as tarot cards. So Merrin swept up the pack, shuffled the cards into it, and dealt three cards faceup, as Sarah had.

The Tower. Death. The Devil. The same cards he had seen in front of Sarah. Merrin frowned, shuffled the cards back together, and dealt again.

The Tower. Death. The Devil.

A chill flowed down his spine. The same cards twice in a row was coincidence—scary, but still a coincidence. But four times? He was about to gather the cards and try again when the door opened and Sarah reentered with a tray of medical supplies. She set it on the table and Merrin put the cards down.

"Take your shirt off," she ordered. "I'll have to clean the wound first, and— What on earth? Your wrist! Your neck! What happened?"

"I had a very strange day," Merrin said, unbuttoning his shirt. "Can you just fix me up?"

He sat back while Sarah clucked and muttered over him. Some of her ministrations hurt, but he bore it in silence. She cleaned all his wounds and cut a bandage for his ear. Her hands were soft on his skin, and he smelled her scent. As she leaned over him to apply the bandage, her shirt fell open slightly, exposing the curve of her breast. Merrin felt himself responding, and he shifted in the hard chair.

"Does that hurt?" she asked, applying the last bit of tape to his ear.

"Not really."

"It will scar, I'm afraid," she said. "You should have come to see me right away."

"I got too busy," he told her, shrugging back into his shirt despite the bloodstains. He decided to change the subject and gestured at the table. "Tarot cards? I didn't know you dabbled in the occult."

With a self-conscious laugh, Sarah set the tray aside and took the chair opposite Merrin's. "I found them here when I arrived. They help pass the time. Do you know what these mean?"

Merrin shook his head. "It wasn't on the curriculum at the seminary."

"The series is read left to right—past, present, future. The Tower means destruction, a complete and total end. Nothing else can come after. That is in the past. Death means transformation, a change from one place or form to another. That is happening now. The Devil means . . . temptation. Especially physical temptation. That is in the future."

Merrin realized his hand had stolen into his crotch, and he casually moved it back onto his thigh. "I wanted to ask you," he said a little too loudly, "did you treat Bession?"

"I tried." Sarah's voice was flat. "There was nothing I could do for him. He had no medical symptoms, nothing to suggest any kind of disease or infection. His breakdown was purely mental. And extremely severe."

"How severe?"

"He spent two days in the hospital here. By the end of the second day, he was foaming at the mouth and I had to get Chuma and Emekwi to restrain him."

"And that's why the Turkana fear the church is cursed."

"That, and the disappearances."

Merrin cocked his head. "Disappearances?"

"No one told you?"

"I'm getting the feeling no one tells me anything," Merrin said.

Sarah smiled. She had a dimple, and Merrin found

it thoroughly endearing. "In the past few weeks since the church was uncovered, we've lost a dozen men."

"Lost. You mean they ran away?" He gestured at the cards and added a sarcastic note to his voice. "Or was it those evil spirits?"

"Yes," Sarah said with a small laugh that sounded forced to Merrin's ear. Then she fell silent. Merrin couldn't think of anything to say, but he didn't feel uncomfortable about it. It was nice to sit with her. Her bare forearms rested on the table, and Merrin's eye fell on her tattoo. She caught him looking, and he flushed.

"I'm sorry," he said. "I shouldn't—"

"No, your curiosity is perfectly natural." Her fingers drifted down to touch the blue numbers, then stopped before they made contact. "My father was a strong man. When the Nazis started rounding up the Jews, he didn't hesitate. He hid our neighbors in the crawl space. Someone turned us in, and we were sent to the concentration camps. It was . . . well, you know."

"People can't understand, can they?" Merrin said. "If they weren't there, I mean. If they didn't see."

"No. And my husband turned out to be one of them. We came to Africa together, completely in love. One night I realized I had to tell him the truth about . . . about the Nazis . . . what they'd done to me." She paused and cleared her throat. Merrin wanted to reach across the table and take her hand, but his own hands wouldn't move. "It was a big mistake. After I finished, he never touched me again."

Pain creased her face, a pain Merrin knew all too well. He forced his hand to move, touch the back of hers. It was cold. Her eyes found his, and her voice dropped to a whisper.

"It's amazing what you're capable of when your own survival is at stake," she said. "The things you'll endure. The things you'll . . . do."

He nodded. "Is that why you came here?"

"I was drawn here, I guess," she said. "To help these people. I won't give up just because there's trouble." She straightened in her chair and blinked rapidly. Her hand left his. "So. What turns a man of the cloth into an archaeologist?"

"I was an archaeologist first."

Sarah smiled. "That's not an answer."

Her directness caught him by surprise, as did a rising desire to satisfy her curiosity. He liked it that she listened to him, paid attention to him. "I found I needed to work with something real," he said. "Something I could hold in my hands."

"Do you miss it? Being a priest?"

Again, her directness surprised him. This time he looked away, before she could see his own pain. "There's no point in missing it."

"Sometimes I think the best view of God is from hell."

Merrin stared into his lap, considering this. His arousal had died. At last, he said, "I should get to bed." He rose and turned to go, then halted. "I'm leaving for Nairobi in the morning to see Bession."

She looked surprised. "To what end?"

"I need to see if he can tell me anything about the site."

"I wouldn't get my hopes up," she said with an unexpected note of bitterness. "He was drooling when Chuma put him on the lorry."

"I have to try."

"Then you'll want to talk to Father Gionetti. He runs the sanitarium."

"All right. And thank you. For the medical care, I mean."

"Just be sure to pay your bill." She smiled up at him, and her dimple showed again. He found himself smiling back.

"Good night, Doctor," he said.

"Good night," she returned, watching Merrin as he left.

Six

✠

Village of Derati, British East Africa

> *No child should be babied while another is offered to the hyena to bite.*
>
> —Kenyan proverb

KNEELING ON THE hard wooden floor of his room in Emekwi's hotel, Father William Francis recited his evening prayers in a low, soft voice. It was a quiet, comforting ritual he had used to end his day since childhood, and he found it relaxed him, helped him let go of the stress and strain of the day's events. It felt good to lay his problems at God's feet and release his worries, if only for a single night.

Tomorrow he would have to start the mission school. He had a precious handful of books and supplies, and Emekwi was supplying the space. Will had been putting off the project, telling himself he was needed at the dig site and that he needed to get acquainted with the Derati before opening a school for their children. It was true that Merrin's discovery rated attention from the Church, but it was also true that Merrin was far better qualified than Will to handle any artifacts. And he had to admit that the buried church scared the hell out of him.

Was he using the school as an excuse to avoid the place? Will bit his lip. Perhaps. On the other hand, he did have to get the school up and running, and the sooner, the better.

To his annoyance, he found he had stopped praying. Will sighed. This was supposed to be a time to let his problems go until morning, not mull them over further. He opened his eyes and saw the crucifix he had nailed to the wall was upside down.

"*Qui?*" he said, the Latin of his prayers momentarily carrying over into the spoken word. For a moment he flashed back on the giant crucifix dangling from its chain in the depths of the church, and he shivered. Who had done such a blasphemous thing, and how had he done it? More mysteries, more worries. With a slightly shaky hand Will righted the crucifix, blew out the lamp, and climbed into the narrow bed. A soft night breeze eddied in through the mosquito netting that covered the window.

There was a whisper of movement. Will sat bolt upright, his nightshirt tangling around his legs. He stared around the dark room and strained to listen. Nothing but jungle noises in the distance. Will lay back, willing his thudding heart to calm down. The darkness seemed to ooze about him like a hungry panther, ready to pounce and slash through the blankets. Paralyzed with fear, breath coming in little spurts, Will's eyes strained to catch sight of whatever was out there, but he saw only utter blackness. He could strike a match, light the lantern. The matchbox was only a handbreadth away. But that would mean moving, drawing attention to himself.

A faint scraping sound came from the far wall. The hair on Will's neck prickled and his skin went cold. The scraping sound came again. He told himself it was just a mouse or a rat in the wall, but the terror didn't abate. He was being ridiculous, a child afraid of monsters in the dark. But still he couldn't move.

He remembered a time when he was small and just about to climb into bed. A furry claw had shot out from under the bedstead and grabbed his ankle. Will had screamed and screamed, but when his parents came bursting into the room, the culprit had turned out to be his older brother Peter, hiding under the bed with a big woolen mitten. The scraping was certainly something equally mundane, perfectly normal.

The scraping noise stopped, but Will's heart continued to pound. Finally, he lunged for the matchbox and struck a flame. Yellow light flared, driving the shadows to the corners and making them dance there. Will held the match high and scanned the room. Nothing. No monsters, no mice, no rats.

Feeling foolish, Will shook the match out and lay back down. Eventually he drifted off to sleep, unaware that across the room, hidden by shadow, the crucifix once again hung upside down.

• • •

Former Father Lankester Merrin sat on his bed with Bession's drawings spread out around him like a demonic quilt. In the center of them lay the rubbing Semelier had given him. An alarm clock ticked on the nightstand. Merrin stared at the drawings, trying to find a pattern, something that made sense. Nothing came to him. He was about to gather the papers up and go to bed when a noise caught his attention. Standing in the open doorway of the bedroom was the silhouette of a woman. Merrin sat upright.

"Sarah?" he breathed. No response.

A dozen questions swirled in his mind, questions and possibilities. Had she come hoping to share his bed? A part of him was embarrassed at the idea, and a part of him was intrigued, even excited. But it would be breaking his vow of chastity. She had to know that. Maybe she just wanted to talk, talk about the camps. Merrin didn't know if he could bear more of that tonight, though.

The woman opened her palm, revealing a dripping, bloody wound. With a gasp, Merrin tried to get up and go to her, but he found himself tangled in drawings and bedclothes.

"Can't rise to the occasion, priest?" whispered a wet voice in his ear. Merrin twisted and saw a black-uniformed SS officer standing next to him. His collar bore a lieutenant's insignia.

"Kessel?" Merrin said.

The alarm clock ticked. Granville's butterflies fluttered madly in their glass cases, pinned to the boards and unable to move. Merrin wanted to free them, but Kessel was standing at the foot of his bed, a mocking laugh emerging from the wet cave of his mouth.

"If you want her, you have to go through me, priest," Kessel sneered. Behind him, the woman fluttered about, pinned to the wall by her hand. "Come forward. Forward, now."

The ticking of the clock became the tramp of marching boots. A girl, fifteen or sixteen years old, was singing as she skipped down a cobblestoned street. Merrin tried to reach out to her, tell her to run, but he couldn't speak. A cold rain began to fall on a small crowd of villagers huddled in the town square. A troop of armed soldiers kept guard on them.

"You, priest," Kessel snapped. "What is your name?"

"I am Father Merrin," he said, still trying to stand up.

Kessel reached into the group of villagers, yanked out the teenage girl, and pressed a gun to her head. "God is not here today, priest."

"No!" Merrin shouted. But Kessel pulled the trigger.

Merrin jerked awake. Three drawings fluttered to the wood floor like obscene snowflakes. He stared around, wild-eyed. The lamplight was dimming, going out, and the room lay in twilight. The alarm clock ticked its usual rhythm. Everything was normal.

Merrin's breath came short and fast, and his heart pounded hard enough to make his wounded ear throb. He lay among the drawings for a long moment, calming himself. Everything was all right. It was just the usual dream. He started gathering up the papers, then saw Semelier's rubbing. The demonic figure seemed to be staring up at him. Merrin reached for it, then noticed that the alarm clock had stopped ticking.

James took a deep drink from the ladle and dropped it back into the bucket with a small splash. He wasn't really thirsty, but needing a drink was a perfectly legitimate excuse to be out of bed this late at night. Papa said he and Joseph would be up early tomorrow so they could attend the new school. James had mixed feelings about that. On the one hand, school would be something new, and being able to read was a sign of status. On the other hand, it would mean spending the day cooped up inside with Joseph and the new white father. None of the other parents in the village were making their children attend school, but Papa said they would come in time, especially if they saw how much James and Joseph were learning.

Bobo, James's little monkey, dashed out of the hotel and scampered up to the bucket. James filled the ladle and held it down for the animal to drink. James petted Bobo's soft head with a finger, and the monkey let out a screech. James jerked his hand back. Bobo hissed and showed his fangs at something behind James. James whirled—

—and found Joseph standing in the dimly lit doorway.

"I had a bad dream," Joseph said softly.

Bobo screeched again, and James hushed him. Papa wasn't very fond of the monkey, and it wouldn't take much for him to decide Bobo had to go. "It's late," James said in his best older-brother voice. "You should go back to bed."

Joseph gave a violent shake of his head.

"Papa will get mad," James warned.

Joseph shrugged, then glanced down at the boards that made up a rough back porch for the hotel. Lying there was the little rock hammer, the gift of the other white father. Joseph reached down for it, but James was quicker. He snatched it away and, in true big-brother style, held it high above his head. Bobo screeched again. Joseph stood on his toes, reaching for the hammer.

"Give it back!" he shouted angrily. "It's mine!"

James backed into the yard. Bobo hissed at Joseph, who chased after his brother, demanding the hammer back. Finally he started to cry in huge gulping sobs.

"All right, all right," James said, suddenly afraid Joseph would go wake Papa and get them both in trouble. "Go back to bed and I'll give you the stupid thing."

Joseph stopped crying, sniffed hard, and put out his hand for the hammer. Bobo, who was standing between them, hissed. He jumped away from Joseph, leaping for James's shoulder. James didn't follow what happened next, it all came so fast. There was a breath of air, damp and smelling of carrion. A dark and powerful form burst from the dark and snapped up the monkey in midair. Bobo's scream of pain died in a wet crunch.

James took a step backward as the hyena turned

yellow eyes on him. Bobo's mangled corpse hung in shreds from its mouth, and blood pattered the ground under its chin. James could have reached out and patted the beast like a big, friendly dog. He smelled Bobo's blood and bowel. On the other side of the hyena, Joseph made a strangled sound. A terrible cold giggle slid out of the shadows, and a second hyena moved in toward Joseph, its claws click-click-clicking on the hard ground.

"Joseph!" James whispered. "Joseph, look out!"

Joseph saw the second hyena. His breath was coming in quick gasps, and he couldn't seem to move. James wondered if Joseph's body would crunch like Bobo's. But the shaggy animal moved past the younger boy and instead focused on James. Terrified, James backed away and almost bumped into a third hyena. It laughed in his ear, spraying him with gooey saliva and breath that smelled of rotting meat. Warmth ran down James's leg as his bladder let go. The three hyenas paced around him in a slow, lazy circle. Their yellow eyes never left his.

"Get Papa, Joseph," James croaked. "Quick!"

But Joseph stood rooted to the spot. One of the hyenas raised a lightning paw and swiped James's side. Hot pain slashed his body and he screamed. The hyenas whooped and giggled, a high sound that spoke of insanity. James screamed again as the first hyena leaped.

Merrin was out of bed and halfway down the hotel stairs before his mind fully registered what he had heard. He pounded through the kitchen and out the back door, only barely aware that Will Francis was right behind him in a nightshirt.

A terrible scene greeted him. Joseph was staring wide-eyed, only three feet from a trio of hyenas. The animals were tearing at young James. One had pulled his left arm off. Another had taken a bite out of his shoulder. Blood sprayed into the air. James screamed and screamed and screamed.

An explosion slammed through Merrin's bones and the head of one of the hyenas vanished in a cloud of blood and brain. Emekwi stood in the doorway with a shotgun, frantically trying to reload. The bigger of the two remaining hyenas bit down on the top of James's head. Merrin heard a horrible popping sound as the animal's teeth punched through the boy's skull. James stiffened, and his screams stopped. Then the hyenas were off and running, dragging James's body with them. Emekwi raised the shotgun and fired again. He missed. The hyenas ran laughing into the darkness. Emekwi screamed something incoherent and ran after them, brandishing the shotgun.

Stunned, Merrin turned to Joseph just in time to see the boy's eyes roll back in his head. He collapsed to the ground. Operating on pure instinct, Merrin scooped Joseph up and ran for the hospital, not slowing to see if anyone followed him.

Sarah flung the door open just as he arrived. "I heard screams and shots," she said. "What—?"

"Joseph. I think he's in shock," Merrin said. He dashed inside—Sarah had already lit lamps—and lay Joseph on one of the beds. Sarah pushed past Merrin and tried to check Joseph's pupils, but his eyes had rolled back into his head. Next she checked his pulse and examined his face. His lips and gums were turning blue.

"His pulse and breathing are shallow and rapid," she said, "and he is becoming cyanotic. It's shock. Get me those blankets. Now!" Merrin pulled blankets off several nearby beds and covered Joseph up while Sarah elevated his feet and set up an IV bottle. "I don't have any vasodilators. There isn't much I can do except try to rehydrate. What happened to him?"

"Hyenas," Merrin said. "They tore James apart while he watched."

Sarah gulped but didn't stop working on the IV even as the door burst open and Francis stumbled in, still in his nightshirt. "Did you see that, Lankester? He was standing right there, and the hyenas ignored him!"

"I saw," Merrin said. "They were focused on James, that's all. Not particularly abnormal." But even as he said the words, he knew they were lies. Any normal pack of hyenas would have gone after both boys—more to eat, less to share.

"That was more than focused," Francis said emphatically. "They acted as if Joseph wasn't even there."

"And what is that supposed to mean?" Merrin demanded.

"That it's—that there's . . ." He trailed off. "Look, have you noticed anything strange tonight? Anything else, I mean?"

Merrin thought about the dream and the demon drawings and the blood writing. They were certainly strange, but he had the idea that Francis meant something else, something that couldn't be explained by mundane forces.

"No," Merrin said. "Nothing."

Francis looked uncertain. "Are you sure?"

"Have *you* noticed anything?" Merrin countered. Sarah, meanwhile, disinfected the skin on the inside of Joseph's elbow, inserted a metal needle, and attached it to the rubber IV lead. The boy didn't react.

"I . . . I think that . . ." Francis hesitated again under Merrin's hard gaze, then said, "No. I guess not."

"Are you still leaving for Nairobi tomorrow?" Sarah asked.

Merrin nodded. "I have questions to ask Mr. Bession. If you need vasodilators, better give me a list."

Three days later, Merrin entered a low, forbidding building made of bloodred brick and gray stone. A sign out front read, in English, ST. JOHN'S SANITARIUM. The enormous front doors gaped like a hungry mouth.

Merrin entered and allowed the metal doors to boom shut behind him. He kept on moving forward into the entrance area. The last three days had been full of movement for Merrin. First he had moved to pack a suitcase. Then he had moved to drive three days to Nairobi. Now he was moving forward into the asylum. If he kept moving, he didn't have to think. He didn't have to think about the popping noise that James's skull had made. He didn't have to think about the torn limbs and spraying blood. He didn't have to think about Joseph lying unconscious in Sarah's clinic.

He didn't have to think about Emekwi's grief-stricken face.

It was the latter that filled him with the most guilt, in those rare moments when he allowed himself to consider it. Merrin should be offering Emekwi comfort and solace, help shoulder the man's burden of grief. Instead he had fled to Nairobi without even waiting a single day.

But Merrin wasn't a priest anymore, didn't have to comfort the living over the graves of the dead. Will Francis was better suited to it. Let him handle it.

But still the guilt remained.

The entranceway was painted a dull green. A battered desk stood guard near the door, but it was unoccupied. The lighting was dim and oppressive.

"Hello?" Merrin called. His voice echoed.

No one answered. A staircase and several corridors led in various directions. Merrin chose a hallway at random and moved forward. Eventually he came across a black-clad nun, who informed him in a thick Irish accent that the offices were on the first floor and patients were kept on the second.

"Is Father Gionetti here?" Merrin asked her. "I was told I should speak to him."

She made a vague gesture. "He's out and about. If ye wander round long enough, ye'll be sure to find him."

Merrin thanked her and turned to leave.

"Be careful," she called after him. "Ye can enter, but ye can't get out."

Merrin didn't stop to ask for clarification. Instead he climbed the first set of stairs he came across and found himself in front of another set of double doors. He pushed through them. Once he released the doors, they automatically began to swing shut, and only then did Merrin realize what the sister had meant. The doors were levered, and opened only from one side. He lunged, but the door slipped past his fingers. Both doors slammed shut. Merrin tugged on a handle. Locked. He would have to find someone with a key to let him out.

Merrin turned and faced the chamber he had entered. His jaw dropped in shock. Patients, dozens of them, wandered around an enormous common room. All were dressed in loose hospital gowns and slippers— male and female, old and young. Most of the people were white, though perhaps six or seven blacks wandered through the mix. A few rickety-looking tables and ladderback chairs were scattered about. Heavy bars and grates covered the grimy windows. The light was gray, and the air was heavy with the pungent smells of urine and vomit.

Most of the people had empty eyes. Some sat in chairs and stared at their hands or their feet or at nothing at all. Others shuffled about in their slippers, muttering or waving their hands. A young man in a corner opened his mouth wide and flapped his wrists. A gray-haired woman carried on an argument with empty air. A balding white man suddenly leaped onto the back of a black man and pummeled him with his fists. The black man dropped to the gritty wood floor, howling and trying to dislodge his attacker. None of the other patients interfered. Most didn't even seem to notice. Merrin's stomach turned. The assailant abruptly appeared to lose interest. He disengaged and wandered off, growling to himself. The victim remained hunched on the floor like a turtle pulled into its shell.

Merrin finally spotted another nun. She was kneeling on the floor with a bucket of water, scrubbing at something on the boards. He made his way across the room, feeling like a traveler through a circle of hell. The nun looked up as he approached.

"Who are you?" she demanded. This one was Italian, and her accent was so thick that Merrin could barely understand her.

"I'm Fa— I'm Lankester Merrin," he said. "I came from Derati to see Anton Bession. He's a patient here."

"Mr. Bession is down in the chronic wing," she said, pointing at a corridor Merrin hadn't noticed before. "You risk to visit him." And she went back to her scrubbing. The brush hissed against the floor.

Merrin turned to go, then stopped. "Excuse me, but is this place really helping these patients?"

The brush stopped. "Nothing can help these patients. They are lucky to have food and a place to rest their heads at night. Most of the time we have not enough to pay even that."

Merrin nodded. All too often the people who needed the most got the least. More evidence that God didn't care. He stepped smartly down the indicated corridor. Patients hovered like ghosts, some wearing gowns stained with their own filth. Several doors faced the corridor. Each bore a card with a name written on it, though often the handwriting was barely legible.

A young man plucked at Merrin's sleeve. He was

110

dark-haired and handsome. Clear, bottle-green eyes contrasted sharply with his fair skin. He wore brown slacks and a shirt with a collar.

"Please . . . are you a doctor?" he asked timidly.

Merrin shook his head. "I'm a visitor."

"Oh, thank God. You have to help me." He looked around, but the only people in sight were other patients. "I don't belong here. I'm not insane. My brother got me committed because Dad left me most of his estate."

"Really?" Merrin answered in a carefully neutral voice. He looked around, hoping to see a doctor or another nun.

"You don't believe it," the young man said, and tears filled his eyes. "Oh, God—you have to believe me. I'm going nuts in here. Look at me! Do I look like *them?* My name is Danny Walsh. My father was James Walsh. My brother's name is Adrian. He got married last month to a girl named Melissa—*my* girl! It was in all the papers. You can check!"

Merrin wavered. Danny had a point—he didn't look at all like the slack, vacant people around him. He wore clean clothes instead of a filthy gown, and he was clear-eyed and well-spoken.

"Maybe I can talk to the doctor," Merrin said. "Do you know where he is?"

"I'll take you to him," Danny said excitedly. "This way."

He led Merrin back toward the common room. Danny's steps were light and firm.

"Thank you for helping me," he said. "A few more days in the place and I really *will* go insane. God. It's not

111

like I could help what happened to those children."

Merrin stopped. "What children?" he asked casually.

"The ones who wanted me to eat them," Danny replied in a matter-of-fact voice. "I wasn't going to hurt them, anyway . . . just take a couple bites."

Merrin turned and walked back down the corridor, ignoring Danny's heartfelt pleas for him to come back. Eventually they faded. One of the doors he passed shuddered as something slammed into it from the other side. It shuddered a second time, and a third. Then it stopped.

Suddenly Merrin noticed he was alone. The last twenty feet of hallway was empty of people, as if someone had drawn an invisible line they instinctively knew not to cross. He watched an old woman with snarled gray hair shuffle toward him, then veer off. Her toothless mouth worked, silently mouthing words only she could hear, but she wouldn't come any closer.

The door at the end of the corridor had a thick, grimy window. The air around Merrin was growing chilly. His shirt felt too thin, in fact, and the end of his nose felt cool. He checked the card tacked to the door and made out the name Anton Bession in crabbed handwriting. The man was once the Derati site's original chief archaeologist, and now he was here. Merrin peered through the dirty glass of the window. He was just able to make out a man inside, sitting at some kind of desk with his back to the door. Merrin tried the door handle, but it was locked. Of course. Feeling thwarted, he turned to go, intending to look for someone with a key.

A *click* stopped him.

The door had drifted open a crack. That was strange. Maybe Merrin just hadn't pulled hard enough. He hesitated, then poked his head into the room. The smell slammed into him like a physical force. Human waste with overtones of rotting food. It made the main room of the asylum smell like a lilac bush in comparison. Brown smears on the walls testified to part of the stench's source. Fighting to keep his gorge down, Merrin stepped inside.

Ice-cold air washed over Merrin and chilled him instantly. His breath hung in the befouled atmosphere like dirty fog. He stood rooted to the spot in shock and bewilderment. What the hell was going on?

Bession continued to hunch over the desk, hard at work on something Merrin couldn't see. Pictures hung on the walls, stuck there by the filth. More paper demons leered at Merrin. He fished a handkerchief out of his pocket and pressed it to his nose in an attempt to filter out the smell.

"Mr. Bession?" Merrin choked out. Bession didn't respond. His right arm moved, as if he were drawing or writing. "Mr. Bession, you worked on a dig in Derati."

Bession laughed, an icy sound that fit the room. Outside, Merrin heard faint shouts, screams, and the thud of flesh striking flesh. A fight had broken out in the main room. Merrin became acutely aware that he was standing alone in a cell with a madman. He shivered with both cold and unease.

"You drew a picture of an idol," Merrin said. "Where did you see it?"

There was a slow tapping sound from the floor near Bession's desk. Bession continued his work. Merrin didn't know what to do, so he kept talking.

"Was the idol in the church?" he asked. "Mr. Bession?"

"Father Lankester Merrin." The man's voice was hard as stone. Merrin froze and his stomach tightened.

"How do you know my name?" he asked in a hoarse whisper.

The tapping sound picked up speed. A scarlet puddle oozed from under the desk, slow, slick, and shiny. Bession's arm moved faster.

"I said, *how do you know my name?*" Merrin shouted. The door behind him slammed. Bession slowly rose to his feet. He was large and bulky. Merrin backed up a step, then reached behind him and tried the door. Locked. Had one of the other patients . . . ? Bession turned around. The front of his gown was torn to shreds, and he was clutching the front of it together. Blood leaked steadily from between his fingers and streamed down his front.

"You're hurt," Merrin said, knowing how stupid the comment sounded.

"No," replied Bession, his eyes locked onto Merrin's. "I am *free.*" He moved his fists away from his chest, and the bloody remains of his shirt fell open. A bleeding swastika gleamed wetly on his chest. Merrin tried to back away, but his spine already pressed against the freezing cold door. The noise of the fight outside grew into a roar.

"God," Bession said in the voice from Merrin's dream, "is not here today, priest."

The words turned Merrin's knees to water, and he slid down the door to the icy floor. His breath puffed in great clouds, his feet and hands turned numb with cold. Bession opened a dripping fist, revealing a long shard of glass. The tip of Merrin's index finger throbbed. Bession pressed the point of the shard to his own neck. The noise of the fight outside grew into a roar.

"No!" Merrin tried to shout, but it came out as an incoherent croak.

Bession rammed the shard home. It made a faint hiss as it sliced through skin and muscle. Blood spurted, then gushed in a fountain. A wide grin spread across Bession's face, and his arm kept moving, sawing with gleeful precision. Merrin heard a pop and the whistle of escaping air as the glass opened Bession's windpipe. Merrin pushed himself backward as hard as he could, as if he could push himself out through the unyielding door. A scattering of blood, already cold, spattered his face and the drawings, making it appear that the figures were bleeding. A long, gruesome moment later, Bession's legs buckled and he collapsed in a bleeding tangle.

The room went dead quiet, and the roar of the fight outside stopped. Merrin heard nothing but the booming thud of his own heart. Carefully, he pushed himself to his feet and looked down at the mess that had been Bession's neck. Strings of ruined skin and meat hung from the gash, and blood formed a glistening puddle. Nausea oozed through Merrin's stomach, and he threw up. Vomit splattered across the floor. When Merrin was finished, he noticed the room was no longer icy.

His eye fell on a piece of paper poking out from the

shadows pooled around Bession's bed. Merrin wiped his mouth on his sleeve, edged around the twitching body, and picked the paper up. It was a charcoal drawing of a church—*the* church. There were the four Michael statues, though it took Merrin a moment to recognize them—they were near-formless blobs. The crucifix, done in much greater detail, hung upside down just behind them.

The strange thing was that another building was seated on top of the church. It looked like a pre-Christian temple, though the drawing was rough and it was hard to tell. A handful of human figures inside, done in detail like the crucifix, engaged in various sex acts. Merrin frowned, the theological side of his brain shifting into gear despite the gory surroundings. The picture's symbolism was obvious—decadence and pleasure over love and faith. His first instinct was to drop the paper back on the floor, but something else made him roll it up for keeping. He stepped around Bession's body again and reached for the door, expecting it to be locked.

The handle twisted like a frog under his hand. Merrin leaped back. His foot slipped in the vomit and blood that slicked the floor, and he fell heavily against one wall. An old man, bald, hook-nosed and wearing a priest's collar, entered the room. Two white-clad order-lies—natives, by their coloring—hurried into the room. One of them had a swollen eye and the other had dried blood on his nose. They had clearly been involved in the fight outside. Merrin wondered how the nun with the scrubbing brush had fared. The old priest looked down at the mess that had been Anton Bession, then gestured at the orderlies to see to the corpse.

"I hope he finds peace," the priest said. His accent was Italian. He turned to Merrin. "I'm Father Gionetti. I've been waiting for you."

Seven

✠

St. John's Sanitarium, British East Africa

The devil turns against its friend.
— Kenyan proverb

TALL PALM TREES waved gently in a late afternoon breeze scented with flowers. Gravel crunched beneath Merrin's boots as he and Father Gionetti walked a winding pathway behind the asylum. It felt wonderful to be out in the fresh air after the horrors of bedlam. Every step that took Merrin away from the hospital made him feel immeasurably better. Gionetti walked beside him, easily keeping pace despite his advanced age.

"You still haven't told me how you knew I was coming," Merrin said. "Did Sarah somehow contact you?"

"No," Gionetti said. "Rome did."

Merrin stopped. Gionetti didn't notice right away and had to backtrack when he realized Merrin was no longer beside him.

"What? Why?" Merrin demanded. "Why would Rome tell you I was coming down from Derati?"

Gionetti clucked his tongue. "Have you drifted so far from God, Merrin, that you can't see? Monsieur Bession was touched by the devil."

"Demonic possession?" Merrin scoffed. "Father, forgive me, but I can't believe you would think—"

"I never said Bession was possessed," Gionetti interrupted. "Only touched." He resumed walking, and Merrin was forced to move forward to continue the conversation.

"Touched?" Merrin repeated. "What the hell does that mean?"

"In 1647, the Ursuline convent in Loudun, France, was plagued by possession. Thirty-four nuns had been touched by the devil, committing unspeakable acts."

"Yes, yes, I'm familiar with it," Merrin said dismissively. "Urbain Grandier was a handsome scoundrel who seduced the prioress and indulged in orgies with a number of other nuns. One account mentions a goat, but that was probably an exaggeration. It doesn't mean the nuns were possessed—just horny and inventive. Grandier, meanwhile, refused to let Cardinal Richelieu tear down the Castle of Loudun, so Richelieu had a few words with the local prosecutor. Voilà! Grandier was brought up on charges of witchcraft. And the Church, ever merciful, tortured him by crushing his feet and legs to make him confess. When he continued to profess innocence, they burned him alive. It was sex and politics, nothing more."

"The accounts written at the time mention more than sex and politics," Gionetti countered. "Nicolas

120

Aubin, a Protestant pastor in Loudun, wrote that the nuns—I quote now—'struck their chests and backs with their heads, as if they had their necks broken, and with inconceivable rapidity; they twisted their arms at the joints of the shoulder, the elbow, or the wrist, two or three times around.' He goes on to say that the nuns threw themselves backward until their heads touched their feet, and they walked in that position with amazing speed."

"That account has not been proven authentic," Merrin pointed out. "For one thing, it was not written in Aubin's handwriting. And in any case, Aubin was a Protestant with a chip on his shoulder toward Catholics. He's hardly a reliable witness."

"Four priests were dispatched to exorcize the demons," Gionetti continued. "Three of them were possessed themselves and subsequently died. The last one was driven insane by his brush with evil. That is what happened to Monsieur Bession. Evil walks in Derati."

Merrin wanted to laugh in the man's wrinkled face. But then images flashed through his mind. The crucifix hanging upside down. The hyenas ignoring Joseph and tearing James to shreds. The glass shard that pierced Bession's neck. The icy room. He remained silent.

"You must be careful there," Gionetti insisted. "Remember, he is the father of lies. He will seek to poison your mind." He removed a book from his robes and handed it to Merrin. "You will need this against him."

Merrin stopped on the path and looked at the title. *The Book of Roman Rituals*. "The exorcism rituals? I'm no longer a priest."

"You will *always* be a priest, Father Merrin." Gionetti patted his shoulder. "Your faith can save you."

"Then I am doomed," Merrin said, and walked away.

Dr. Sarah Novack stared down at the thick medical book. The sun had set over an hour ago, and the lamps burning on her desk didn't provide nearly enough light. Still, she persevered. Sweat dripped down her forehead, and she paused in her reading to wipe it away. She jotted a note from the book, then went back to reading. The text swam in front of her eyes. Sternly she tried to force her eyes to focus, but they refused to cooperate.

She slammed the book shut and rubbed her face. The strain was telling on her. Joseph had been drifting in and out of consciousness for almost a week now, and Sarah had yet to find a cause, let alone a cure.

The events of that terrible night still haunted her sleep. Emekwi had gone after the hyenas with his shotgun and had returned with his son's bloody, headless remains. The villagers had burned them, according to local custom. Merrin had fled, Francis had closed the school before it even opened, and Joseph remained in Sarah's clinic.

Click-click-clack.

Sarah shot a glance at the open doorway that led into the clinic proper. A shadow glided past, accompanied by the clicking of claws on wood. She caught a whiff of rotten meat. Adrenaline spurted through her and she forced herself to get quietly to her feet. Her hand found a scalpel on the desk. Not much of a weapon, but better than nothing. She ghosted to the door and peered into the clinic beyond.

Darkness dimmed her vision, but she was able to

make out shapes. It occurred to her that she was backlit by the lamp in the room behind her, so she eased around the doorjamb into the main room. Her heart pounded in her ears. Any moment she expected to sense hot breath on her body, feel teeth pop through her skin and skull. Her eyes adjusted to the low light and she scanned the clinic. No hyenas in sight. So what had made the—

Joseph's bed was empty. Nerves humming, she moved closer. The sheets and blanket were rumpled. The tube from the IV bottle dribbled fluid from the needle, which lay on the floor. Something moved on the other side of the bed. Scalpel in hand, Sarah forced herself to ease around it and look.

The boy was sitting on the floor, facing away from her. A blanket covered an object in his lap. His fingers moved beneath the cloth, stroking the object. The boy rocked in place, crooning a little song. Sarah glanced around the room again. Nothing.

"Joseph?" she said quietly. "What do you have there?"

He rocked and crooned some more without answering, or even looking up. That was when Sarah noticed the bloodstains on the blanket. Kneeling on the floor, she twitched the blanket aside. James's bloody head stared up at her. Tooth marks had punctured his forehead.

"It's mine," Joseph said. "He's mine now."

Sarah jolted up from her pillow, heart pounding hard. The dream hung in the air before her, palpable and real. She could almost smell the blood. But it was only a dream. She sighed, turned over—

—and looked straight into Jefferies's oozing face. She screamed and shoved herself backward against the wall. He was kneeling next to the bed, had been breathing into her face.

"You threw it away," he said like a petulant child. The St. Joseph medal he had put around her neck dangled from one fist. "You tossed it like a piece of garbage."

"Get the hell out of here!" Sarah barked, holding the blanket up to her neck.

"It was in the dirt outside," Jefferies continued as if she hadn't spoken. "Why did you throw it away?"

"I didn't." Sarah tried to back away, but she was already against the wall and there was no place to go. Cold fear clutched her heart. "The clasp must've come loose."

"Liar!" he snapped.

She flinched. Automatically her eyes darted about the room, looking for a weapon, any weapon. Although she kept the clinic spotlessly clean, her personal living quarters hovered at the edge of slovenly. On the bedside table beside her empty dinner plate lay a knife. Behind it was a wedding photo in a heavy silver frame. She tensed to lunge for the knife, but Jefferies climbed up on the bed. The springs squeaked beneath him.

"Do I repulse you that much?" he said. Spittle sprayed her face. "Maybe if you could cure my fucking skin, I might look as good to you as that archaeologist."

A scream tore through the air. Jefferies spun around on the bed. Joseph stood in the doorway, eyes wide, looking like a ghost in his sweat-stained nightshirt. He raised a shaking hand and pointed at Jefferies.

"He's coming for you," Joseph said in a harsh whisper.

"What?" Jefferies gasped, clearly unnerved.

"He's coming for you! Coming for you! COMING FOR YOU!" The words came out as a howl. Jefferies bolted from the bed and stumbled out the door. Sarah stared at Joseph, hyperalert to every detail. Joseph was barefoot, and the whites of his eyes were yellow. A few crumbs of bread were scattered across her dinner plate. In the distance, she heard drums begin to beat.

"Joseph," she said, opening her arms to him. "You're awake!"

"I had a bad dream." He ran forward and hugged her. Tears ran down his cheeks. "It was a very bad dream."

Sarah held him close while he cried. Then she noticed the sores on his body.

The sea of white crosses shone in the moonlight as Merrin passed them in the jeep. They gave him a sense of foreboding, as if the graves were a restless army about to awaken. Then he forced himself to pay attention to his driving. It wasn't a good idea to drive after dark, but he was almost to Derati and didn't want to spend another night on the road.

He reached the outer edge of the village, where the huts stood guard against the inner buildings. The night air was warm and dry, and he heard drums beating. Two figures emerged from between the huts and waved at Merrin in the jeep's headlights. Merrin pulled over, and the figures resolved themselves into Chuma and a teenage girl Merrin didn't know. The girl had a medicine vial in her hand. Chuma spoke to her in Turkana. She nodded and vanished into the shadows. Chuma climbed into the jeep.

"Where is everyone?" Merrin asked, putting the jeep back into gear and driving farther into town.

"Sebituana's baby is coming," Chuma said. "The village has gathered in welcome. Except the labor isn't going well, and Sebituana's wife, Lokiria, is in much pain. The girl was Felashaday, the midwife's apprentice."

"Oh?"

"Bititi—the midwife—sent her to fetch medicine from the lady doctor."

"Why doesn't Lokiria come to the clinic?" Merrin asked. "Or Sarah go to Lokiria?"

"Sebituana does not trust western medicine," Chuma replied. "This must remain a secret."

The jeep pulled up in front of the clinic. Merrin climbed out of the vehicle and went inside while Chuma drove off in a puff of dust and exhaust fumes. Lamps burned in the clinic's main room, casting bright light everywhere. Merrin was surprised to see Sarah up and about, though the dark circles under her eyes worried him. Still, he was glad to see her. She was standing next to Joseph's bed, just as she had been doing when he left for Nairobi. For an eerie moment, Merrin wondered if she had moved from that spot in the seven days he'd been gone. She heard Merrin come in and hurried over.

"You're back," she said.

"How's Joseph?" Merrin asked.

Sarah hesitated. "Odd," she said at last. "Come see."

The boy tossed and turned on his bed. The rubber lead still ran from his arm to a glass IV bottle that hung upside down above him. He was covered in sweat, and when he shifted one more time, Merrin leaned forward. Angry red lesions covered Joseph's neck and shoulders. They reminded Merrin uncomfortably of Jefferies's face. Troubled, he pulled the blanket back up.

Joseph's eyes popped open, wide and white. Startled, Merrin pulled back. "Joseph?" he asked. But the boy's eyes had already closed again. Outside, the drumming continued in a bone-throbbing rhythm. Merrin turned to Sarah.

"Are *you* all right?" he said.

She shrugged. "Just tired. He's been like this all week."

"These lesions—they can't just be from the shock of what happened to James."

"We really shouldn't talk here," Sarah said. "Come."

She led Merrin away from the bed, down to the other end of the lamplit room. With a concerned expression she sank down on one of the other beds. "The lesions are completely asymptomatic. It doesn't make any sense. He should have recovered by now. Instead, his blood pressure's dropped and he's running a fever."

"What could it be?"

"In this part of the world?" Sarah gestured at the front door and, by extension, the continent beyond. "A dozen things. But his symptoms don't exactly match any of them. All I can do is watch and wait."

A moment passed. Drums throbbed and pounded. Merrin realized he was staring at Sarah, at her blue eyes and soft, lovely face. She looked back at him, and he found himself hoping she thought him handsome. Unpriestly thoughts. The book Gionetti had given him weighed heavily in the pocket of his trousers.

"I have some work to do at the dig site early in the morning," he said to break the silence. "I should go to bed. Will you be all right?"

She gave him a tired smile, then patted the hospital bed beside her. "Come sit with me, Lankester. I promise I won't bite."

Merrin was all set to refuse, to walk quickly away, but his body sank to the bed beside her. A fly landed on his arm, and he waved it away.

"So how was Nairobi?" Sarah asked, still smiling. "Did you see . . . Monsieur Bession?"

"He's dead," Merrin said flatly.

"What?" Her smile died. "How?"

Merrin regretted his harsh tone, regretted he had killed her smile, but couldn't bring himself to apologize. "He killed himself. Right in front of me."

"Oh God." Sarah put a hand to her mouth. "I don't understand. He was my . . . I can't believe he would . . . God. What happened to him? . . . What's happening to Joseph? . . . I can't seem to help anyone anymore."

Tears gathered in her eyes, and it hurt Merrin's heart to see them. He produced a handkerchief, put an arm around her shoulders, and gently wiped her eyes. Her body was warm under his arm, and he smelled her unique scent. A tendril of brown hair tickled his nose. She leaned a little toward him, and he never wanted to move again. Her hand stole up to his face, and it tingled where she touched. He leaned hesitantly forward, heart keeping beat with the drums. What if he was mistaken? What if she didn't want him to touch her? What if—

She leaned in and kissed him. Her mouth was soft on his. Merrin's head sang. But a strange feeling plucked at him like a ghostly hand. He pulled away.

In the clinic behind them, unseen, a puff of blood clouded Joseph's IV tube.

Merrin discovered he didn't like pulling away and leaned back in. Sarah smiled and they kissed again. She ran her hands over Merrin's chest and the hard muscles of his stomach. Passion roared within him, and he had to fight to keep from pushing Sarah down on the bed.

One of the wheels on Joseph's bed began to turn. It made a slow revolution, squeaking just loud enough for Merrin to hear it. The wheel squeaked again, and this time he broke away from Sarah. Joseph's bed had moved away from the wall.

"What the hell?" he said, rising. Sarah got up with him. They moved quickly across the room to see what was going on. Blood had colored the entire IV bottle.

"I don't understand this at all," Sarah said.

Monsieur Bession was touched by . . .

"No," Merrin said firmly.

"What?"

"Nothing." Merrin put out a hand and laid it on Joseph's forehead—

—and the boy's body leaped from the bed. Merrin jerked back as Joseph went into full-body convulsions. His arm snapped out and the IV bottle crashed to the floor. Shattered glass and bloody fluid cascaded across the wood. Sarah tried to grab him, but the convulsions shook her off.

"Help me hold him!" Sarah shouted. "I can't—"

The convulsions ended. Joseph lay on the twisted bedclothes, his breathing deep and even, as if nothing had happened at all.

Sarah did a quick vitals check, then pursed her lips and said with an edge of hysteria, "What's going on here, Lankester?"

Merrin's mouth became a hard, straight line. He didn't have an answer for her, but he suspected where one was hiding.

Felashaday ran through the dark streets of Derati, the precious vial clutched tightly in her hand. Chuma had offered to drive her, but she had refused. She couldn't afford to look like she had accepted any help from the whites or the people who worked for them. The birth drums pounded out their familiar rhythm, and she matched her steps to their beat.

From the rounded hut ahead of her, Lokiria's groans sounded like a wounded spirit keening for release. Felashaday paused long enough to snatch a handful of palm fronds and wrap them around the precious vial. Outside the hut, a group of elders, including Sebituana, stood in a ring of torches, looking concerned. Nearby, a group of musicians played the childbirth song on flute and drum. The song was supposed to calm the child and call it into this world, but Lokiria's cries nearly drowned them out. Felashaday prayed the white doctor's drugs would help ease Lokiria's pain.

Felashaday was about to enter the hut when Sebituana caught her by the arm in a hard wooden grip. "You have come from the western woman's sick house," Sebituana said. "You taint yourself and our child with your presence. You may not enter."

"I passed by the sick house, Revered Elder," Felashaday confessed, "but I did not enter. Bititi sent me for more herbs."

"Let me see."

Lokiria groaned again. She needed something for the terrible pain, but this brute of a husband wouldn't allow it. How could he, a man, understand the pain of child-birth and how terrible it could be? But he was Lokiria's husband and the elder, which meant no one could gain-say him. Heart pounding, Felashaday held up the palm fronds, hoping that in the dim light Sebituana wouldn't recognize them right away. He narrowed his eyes in sus-picion and Lokiria's heart sank.

"Those look like—"

"There you are!" snapped a new voice. Bititi had stuck her head out of the hut. "Bring those herbs in, girl. Now!"

Felashaday nipped inside the hut before Sebituana could protest and gave an inward sigh. In here she was safe. Not even Sebituana would enter a childbirthing hut.

The rounded hut was normal-sized, long enough for two people to lie end to end across the middle and tall enough for a man to stand erect in the center. A flexible wooden frame supported thickly woven palm fronds. A hole in the roof let out the smoke from a small fire. Near the fire, an older woman helped Lokiria remain on her feet. Lokiria was young and very pretty, with glossy skin, hair woven into dozens of plaits, and soft brown eyes. She was naked, and Felashaday saw muscle ripple across her distended stomach. Lokiria's face was clenched with pain.

Felashaday handed the palm fronds to Bititi, the gray-haired midwife, and went over to help the other assistant keep Lokiria on her feet. The white doctor usually had women give birth lying down, something Felashaday didn't agree with, despite the power of western medicine in other areas. It made much more sense for the mother to stand up so the earth could help draw the baby forth.

"Praise the ancestors," Bititi said in a voice that would not carry outside the hut. "This will help her."

Lokiria screamed again. Felashaday bit her lip. The sound made her hair stand up, made her want to run and hide with her fingers in her ears. She scolded herself to grow up. At age sixteen, Felashaday had assisted Bititi with over a dozen births now, and all of the women had screamed. But these screams had a different quality. The other women had screamed to release the pain. Lokiria screamed because there was nothing left for her to do. Felashaday's blood chilled every time she heard it.

Bititi, meanwhile, poured some of the white doctor's "mor-feen" into a cup, added goat's milk, and was holding it to Lokiria's mouth for her to drink when a hand slapped the cup away. It tumbled hissing into the fire. Sebituana, his face angry as a thundercloud, glared down at Bititi. He did not look at his wife. Felashaday shrank back, aghast and frightened at seeing a man in this place. Sebituana snatched the vial from Bititi's hand

and, ignoring his wife's screams of agony, crushed it beneath his sandaled foot.

"Bad medicine," he growled. "You will not poison my wife!"

Lokiria screamed again as Sebituana stalked out of the hut.

Merrin stood on the roof of the church. Overhead, the full, ripe moon shed enough silver light to read by, which was exactly what Merrin was doing. He had unrolled Bession's drawing of the double church and was now pacing the boundaries of the roof.

A frown crossed Merrin's face. If Bession had meant the drawing to be literal instead of metaphorical, and if there had at one time been a second church on top of this one, there would be signs of it—support columns, specially reinforced walls, *something*. Yet Merrin saw nothing.

He rerolled the drawing and slid it into his back pocket. It stuck out like a holder for candy floss. He drew aside the piece of canvas that covered the dome and peered into the depths of the church. From his backpack he pulled what looked like a bundle of rope with a pair of hooks on one end. He set the hooks against the lip of the dome and tossed the bundle into the darkness. The rope ladder he had bought in Nairobi unrolled without a hitch. Merrin donned his pack again and climbed carefully down.

It was like descending a shaft of moonlight. The ladder swung and twisted within the silvery beam that lit his descent. He reached the bottom and stepped onto the hard marble floor. A menace of shadows greeted him.

A part of Merrin called himself an idiot for coming

out here alone at night—night was when the demons and devils came out to play. Then his more rational self pointed out that the church was dark inside whether it was day or night out, and that the incident with Bession—*if* demons were involved—had happened during broad daylight. It didn't prevent a certain amount of nervousness from making his skin shiver.

A low muttering croaked in the dark. The hair on Merrin's neck slowly rose. From his backpack he pulled a lantern and lit it with his lighter. One of the St. Michael statues was covered with crows again, easily twice as many as before. They blinked at him with fierce yellow eyes.

Something on the ground at the statue's feet caught Merrin's attention, and he moved the light downward. The sight made his stomach churn with queasiness. A dozen crow bodies, dismembered and pecked for meat, lay scattered on the floor. Blood, feathers, and loops of bowel were everywhere. Their eyes had been gouged out, leaving little holes in the heads about the size left by the hyena who had punched through James's head. The puddle of light cast by the lantern flickered—Merrin's hand was shaking. He forced himself to calm down. Lots of animals were cannibals. Chickens, for heaven's sake, ate their own kind. And crows never flew at night. Merrin was in no danger of attack.

Cautiously, he moved between the archangel statues toward the dais. The crows on the statue shifted and croaked but showed no inclination to leave their perches. Still, Merrin could feel a hundred pairs of sharp avian eyes on him as he set the lantern on the altar and unrolled Bession's drawing. The enormous crucifix still hung upside down, and it seemed as if the upcast eyes of Jesus were fixed on Merrin's paper.

Merrin examined the drawing, then looked up to compare it with the church. It didn't look quite right somehow. But there it was on the paper—the four statues, the upside-down crucifix, the demon temple on top of—

Upside down. The crucifix was upside down. But the break on the base was fresh, meaning the crucifix was originally meant to be right side *up*. With a cold certainty, Merrin turned the drawing around so the second temple was *beneath* the church.

His earlier nervousness vanished beneath a thrill of discovery. He stashed the drawing in his backpack and used the lantern to examine the altar carefully. Mosaics gleamed in the soft light. Angels, some with eight or ten wings instead of the usual two, brandished swords, spears, maces, staves, and even knives. Most Byzantine mosaics portrayed angels as beautiful and serene, but these angels were royally pissed off. Some of them looked straight at Merrin, and he thought of Sarah's kisses with guilt.

Was that where it had started with Urbain Grandier in that French convent three centuries ago? A pair of kisses stolen from the prioress, followed by obsession and hysteria? Maybe Merrin should confess to Francis when this was over, just to be safe. Maybe he should—

He firmed his jaw. Confession was stupid. God knew what he did, what had been done to him, and God clearly didn't give a shit. Why confess when no one cared?

A cold draft wafted across Merrin's face. He set the lantern back down and pulled out his lighter again.

Flicking it on, he passed it back and forth in front of the altar until he found the spot where the flame wavered and danced like a miniature elemental fire. Merrin's questing fingers found a seam near the top of the altar. He put the lighter away, then set the lantern on the floor so it cast light on the altar. From his backpack he took a crowbar. The archaeologist in him screamed blasphemy, but he inserted the tool into the seam and heaved.

Eight

✠

Village of Derati, British East Africa

Whoever leans on a rotting body lacks no flies.
— Kenyan proverb

LOKIRIA GAVE ANOTHER agonized cry. Squatting beneath her, Bititi held out her arms, ready to receive the baby. Felashaday and the other assistant continued to hold her up. Lokiria was tiring, and her weight dragged more and more on Felashaday's aching arms and shoulder.

"Push now," the midwife ordered. "Push hard!"

Lokiria gritted her teeth and obeyed.

"Here it comes," Bititi said, a note of relief in her voice. "I can see the baby's head. You will be a mother soon. Push, now! Push! Here it comes!"

The infant slithered free—and Bititi screamed. She dropped the baby onto the mat between Lokiria's ankles and screamed again. The afterbirth came down in a steaming lump. Lokiria began to sob. Confused, Felashaday helped her to lie down.

"Where's my baby?" Lokiria cried. "Where's my child?"

Bititi had backed away. Her eyes were wide and she was panting. Felashaday glanced down. Her hand flew to her mouth and she stifled a scream of her own. The infant was clearly dead, and its body writhed white with maggots. More maggots spattered Lokiria's loins. The afterbirth crawled with them. The terrible sweet smell of rotten meat filled the hut. Lokiria sat up and saw what was wrong. She screamed as well.

The palm fronds covering the opening to the hut burst aside as Sebituana shoved his way inside. Sebituana's eyes fell immediately upon the decayed body of his son. His face went ashen, then stony with rage.

"The white invaders!" the elder howled. "The white invaders have done this!"

The top of the altar came free with a shriek that sounded like a human scream. Merrin managed to shove it askew far enough to shine his lantern into the black hole beneath. A stone staircase led downward.

Merrin climbed over the wall of the altar and started down the stairs. The stone was older, more roughly carved. At the bottom, the stairs ended in an antechamber the size of a large closet, though it was more a cave than a room. The walls were desert dry. Opposite the stairs was a great round rock, like a lazy

Susan turned on its side. Letters were carved around the outer rim of the rock, and an arcane design in the center twisted Merrin's eye. It felt like the entire weight of the church above was pressing down on him, and he could feel the accusatory weapons of the archangels pointing a warning.

Merrin ran his lantern over the circular stone, trying to read the language. It looked like Greek, the main language of the Byzantine Empire. Squinting in the bad light, he was barely able to make out the names of Emperor Justinian and Empress Theodora.

"So, Your Imperial Majesty," Merrin said aloud. "You ordered this place built. But why?"

His words filled the eerie silence around him and made him feel less alone, so he continued talking, filling the dark void with the sound of his own voice.

"Fairly standard symbolism, Your Majesty," he said, still examining the round stone. "Let's see. The opening at the top of the steps is round, and the altar above it is a square. Down here we have a round rock sealing what I'm going to guess is a square door. The circle combined with a square is a standard symbol of protection. The question is, are you protecting yourself or whatever's hidden down here?"

He shone the lantern at the floor to the left of the round rock. There was a groove in the floor. The rock was meant to roll aside.

"With Your Majesty's permission," Merrin said. He set the lantern down, laid hold of the rock, and pushed. After some initial resistance, it rolled smoothly aside and revealed a square entrance to another cave. Heart pounding behind his ribs, Merrin took up the lantern again and stepped across the threshold.

A wide, empty space echoed before him. Merrin shone his beam around and paled. It was a cave, a natural one that had been expanded—and carved. The wall carvings were more primitive than the mosaics in the church above, and they sent chills down Merrin's spine.

Demons leered at him from every angle. Scenes of nightmare cruelty twisted their way down every wall. The demons were torturing humans—men, women, and children. Here a devil carefully clawed open a screaming woman. There a devil with barbs on its erection sodomized a young man. A child hung by its hair while a demon torturer sliced off its ears. A man and a woman, presumably the child's parents, were forced to watch. An old woman was being strangled by her own entrails. A young woman was being sawed in two. They reminded Merrin of Bession's drawings.

Some of the carvings showed human carnal lust. Men penetrated women in every possible orifice and from every possible position. Groups of three and four and five climbed over each other, their faces leering masks of desire. One man knelt to perform simultaneous fellatio on two other men. A group of four women used fingers, tongues, and carved penises to pleasure each other. Everywhere Merrin looked, he saw horror and pain mix with lust. It brought a sick feeling to the pit of his stomach.

Several sets of chains and shackles hung from the walls. A series of stone tables stood to one side. Merrin ran his lantern light over them. Metal instruments gleamed, unrusted in the dry air. Serrated knives, hooks, spikes, pliers, pincers, tongs, and other objects Merrin couldn't identify. Dark streaks stained most of them.

"Jesus, Mary, and Joseph," he whispered. "What were you doing down here, Your Majesty? Or were you sealing in what someone else did?"

Merrin's lantern continued to sweep the room. The light picked out a stone block in the center of the room. The block had a slight tilt to it. Merrin edged closer to get a better look. His footsteps echoed, and the stony eyes of the demons seemed to follow him. He discovered that it was worse when the demon carvings lay in darkness—the demons could see him, but he couldn't see them.

A flicker of movement caught his eye. He spun and aimed his lantern, but it made a fizzing sound and went out, plunging the entire temple into darkness.

"Shit!" he said.

Something skittered past, and Merrin felt something brush his ankle. A rat? A snake? He bit back a scream and shook the lantern. Nothing. He had filled it with oil. What the hell was—

The light burst back to life. A monster loomed over Merrin, reaching for him with sharp claws. He yelped and almost dropped the lantern. It took him a moment to realize it was only a statue carved into the cave wall. He tried a laugh, but it came out as a high-pitched squeak.

"Just carved stone," Merrin said. "Nice work, Your Majesty."

He stepped forward and peered at the statue, as if to prove he hadn't been in the least afraid, though no one

141

else was around. The figure showed a naked man with the stylized head of a snarling lion, or perhaps a dog. Four wings spread to a span of eight or nine feet. The statue's penis was a curled serpent. A recess had been carved into the statue's abdomen. Merrin stared at it. In the back of the cavity, another figure had been carved into the rock. It was an exact copy of the idol from Semelier's rubbing. Merrin put his hand into the recess and felt the chilly stone. It was as if the niche had been carved so the idol would be pressed into the cavity facing inward, like a key going into a lock. But where was the idol itself? Semelier wasn't going to be happy if it was missing.

"Did you order it brought back to Byzantium, Your Majesty?" Merrin asked aloud. It felt good to hear a human voice, even if it was just his own. "Perhaps Bession stole the stupid thing, eh?"

Merrin pulled back a bit from the statue, and his eye fell on the tilted stone block in the center of the room again. Letters had been carved into the floor, forming a counterclockwise spiral that circled inward toward the block, which appeared to be an altar. Merrin's sense of direction told him it lay directly beneath the four statues in the church above. The altar down here, however, was festooned with the remains of devices for restraint—chains, shackles, and rotted leather cuffs. A pit gaped at the lower end, and the stone surface was heavily grooved.

Looming above the altar were three carved stone images. One was a man with perfectly chiseled muscles and a heavy penis. Another was a woman with large, high breasts and ample hips. Both figures sported fangs and bat wings. The third figure stood between the other two, its arms around their waists. It was also male, heavily muscled, with an enormous erection. It looked like the Devil card from Sarah's tarot deck. Merrin's groin tightened, despite his aversion to the scene.

"This is another temple, isn't it, Your Majesty?" Merrin said, trying to get his mind off his stirring genitals. "Older than the one above. The people of your empire found this one, added to it, and then much later built the church above." He squatted so the lantern light illuminated the spiral of words. "I recognize this, Your Majesty. It's pure Byzantine magic. You chant the words as you walk the spiral inward, and when you reach the center, the spell is cast. What was it supposed to do?"

He stood and shone the lantern on the stone block again. "Those are bloodstains. Your Majesty's people made sacrifices here. Human sacrifices. Did you know about it and make them stop? Or did you . . . discourage it?" Merrin examined the grooves more closely. "I see how it works. The channels let the blood drip down into that pit, which feed the demon or the god or whatever it was. Almost like a scene out of the Inquisition. Of course, you missed all that. You had other problems."

A tickle on his hand made him look down. A fly was crawling over his fingers. He turned his hand over and saw three more. A strange sound hissed near his feet, and he felt something brush his ankle again. Both ankles. He brought the light down.

The floor crawled with flies. Billions of them, covering every flat surface. The hissing sound was their bodies sliding over each other. They coated the ground ankle-deep in a glittering, moving carpet. Merrin had time to gasp before buzzing exploded all around him.

Sarah moved through the clinic, attending to various small tasks without straying more than a few yards from Joseph's bed. Outside, Trenton Jefferies watched her through the clinic window, checking the outline of her body, her rounded ass, her gorgeous tits. The darkness hugged him close, protecting him from view like a friendly blanket. The night air was dry and chilly, devoid of scent. Maybe she'd bend over, or lift her dress to scratch someplace private.

A fly crawled down his face, weaving a pathway among the boils, but Jefferies didn't even notice. He was breathing hard, in danger of fogging the glass. His dick was rock hard, and it made a tent in his pants. He knew from experience that if he touched it, he'd explode, so he left it alone for now. How many white puddles had he left under Sarah's window? Jefferies had lost count. Stupid cunt probably hadn't even noticed. Her snide comments and little jabs were all designed to make him feel stupid and little, but he was all man, sweetheart. He could jerk it three times a day if he wanted to, and make it last with a woman all night.

Problem was, there weren't many real women around. Jefferies didn't count the fuzzies. The idea of stuffing it to one of them made his skin crawl. But Sarah—now *there* was a woman. Soft and pale and white, white, white. And broken in. He had seen the number tattooed on her arm, and he'd heard what the

Nazis did to women in the camps, oh yes. Sarah would be broken in good, and that would make it wonderfully easy to slip it to her, pound her hard. And she'd be *used* to it. Fantastic.

An image of Sarah tied to an examination table stole into his mind. Yeah. Shackled naked, her pink nipples standing up and ready, with a big blond Nazi soldier standing at attention with a big Nazi hard-on bulging in his pants—just like Jefferies's. The doctor in his white coat talking into a reel-to-reel tape recorder: "Now ve check ze subject's sexual rrrresponses. Corporal Schmidt vill assist."

Jefferies pressed his crotch against the clinic wall and stifled a groan at the friction it caused to the underside of his dick. In his head, Sarah was begging Corporal Schmidt not to follow orders, but he was already unbuttoning his fly to release a cock the size of a battering ram. Jefferies reached for his own crotch.

The front door opened and Emekwi walked silently into the clinic. Sarah had her back to the entrance and didn't see him. Emekwi moved closer, and still Sarah didn't realize he was there. Jefferies's mouth opened. He was almost panting, and he forced himself to keep quiet—the window was open a crack and they might hear him. Was Emekwi going to grab Sarah from behind? Do some rear-ending? God, what a sight *that* would be. Some of the fuzzies had bloody big tonkers. Sarah wouldn't be able to take it, big Nazis or not, and Jefferies would hear her cry out with the pain of getting stuffed with some African sausage.

The fly continued crawling around his face, and

Jefferies felt the tickle. He waved the insect away. It buzzed around his head a few times, then landed again. This time Jefferies ignored it. He popped open the top button of his pants.

To Jefferies's disappointment, Emekwi stopped by Joseph's bed. Sarah apparently heard something because she spun in place, her face a mask of surprise. When she saw it was Emekwi, she calmed down and spoke. Jefferies listened hard, barely catching the words through the window's narrow opening.

"Emekwi," she said, but he didn't respond. "I'm doing everything I can for him."

Emekwi left without saying a word.

Jefferies crept to the corner of the clinic building and peered around in time to see Emekwi drag away down the boardwalk, a broken man. Jefferies didn't get it—these fuzzies threw more kids than a mongrel bitch dropped puppies. Why was he getting upset over just one? Well, two, if you counted the one eaten by those hyenas.

His face itched again. He pawed at it, but the itching didn't go away. It never went away entirely, but Jefferies had flare-ups that were worse than the norm. Maybe he was due for another. The itch grew stronger, and Jefferies scratched hard. Something broke under his nails and he felt warm fluid trickle down his cheek. The itch changed to a hot, runny pain. Jefferies wiped his hand on his trousers. Bitch wouldn't even examine him, let alone try to cure him. And now his bottle of scotch was empty. God, he needed a drink. A drink and a blow job. Fuck her. "Fucking cunt," he said.

Jefferies wandered down the boardwalk, more or less following Emekwi back to the hotel and its attached bar. Emekwi, however, passed the darkened building and kept on walking. Jefferies waited until the grieving man's wooden footsteps had faded, then tried the bar's front door, expecting to find it locked. It opened under his hand.

Jefferies found the bar dark and empty. He thought about trying to strike a light, then decided to leave it for a fuck-all. He moved toward the bar at the back of the room. The fly buzzed around his head again, and he waved it away. How the hell was it seeing to follow him in the dark, anyway?

A figure loomed out of the dark ahead of him. Jefferies jumped before he realized it was only his reflection in the dim mirror behind the battered bar. He moved around behind the counter, scanning the low shelves for liquor, but they were empty. He checked underneath the bar, feeling along the splintered shelf. Also empty. No wonder Emekwi hadn't locked the fucking place.

A scritching noise made him jerk upright. Again he came face-to-face with his own reflection in the mirror. The scritching grew louder, like tiny claws edging along a hard surface. The lighting was dim—moonlight that filtered through the open door and cracks in the shutters—but Jefferies saw the movement just before he felt it. One of his sores bulged and moved. He could feel something squirming against the meat of his face beneath the skin.

Nausea bubbled in his stomach. He raised a hand

and, in a gesture he had performed hundreds of times, he plunged a ragged fingernail into the soft surface of the boil. The sore split, and thin fluid burst from it. Then the halves of damaged skin moved like a blanket on a bed, and out crawled a large, black fly.

Jefferies stared in horror, unable to move. The fly's wings were wet. It fluttered them, spraying more fluid, then casually flew away.

Abruptly Jefferies felt more squirming against his face. Inside every boil, a tiny six-legged figure moved. The bar door slammed shut by itself. Trenton Jefferies began to scream.

Flies crawled over Merrin's body, slid into his nose, burrowed into his ears. He clapped his hands over his face, grinding several insects against his skin and trapping a host of others. They buzzed desperately against his fingers. The lantern dropped to the floor. Flies crawled into his clothing and skittered over his bare skin. Their tiny claws were cold. Merrin turned and stumbled toward the exit, hoping he was going in the right direction.

"Help!" he shouted, and flies flew into his mouth. He tried to spit them out, but more came in. Merrin tripped and landed prone among the carpet of flies. They covered him in an instant, crawling into his collar, up his sleeves, down his trousers. His hands and face were black with them. He couldn't see, couldn't hear, couldn't—

His hand touched hot metal. The lantern! Merrin snatched it up. Flies pinged off it, hissing on the sizzling sides. Merrin got to his feet and ran for the square door, pushing through the flies as if they were a living curtain. Somehow he made it. Panting and spitting flies, Merrin rolled the round rock back into place, shutting the door. There was a crunching sound as it rolled over thousands of insects.

The floor of the entranceway at the bottom of the stairs looked perfectly normal. No flies. Merrin shook his clothes, shedding hundreds of tiny black bodies. Finally he gave up and stripped, removing every stitch. He shook out each article of clothing with great care. Live flies rose in clumps and fled up the stairs into the church. Dead ones showered the floor. Merrin could still feel their tiny claws skittering over his chest and stomach, but he saw none on himself. He ran his hands over his skin to make sure, and felt filthy. He desperately wanted a shower or a bath. A pair of flies crawled over his penis. He waved them away, oddly embarrassed, and started pulling on his clothes again. Once everything was in place, he climbed the stairs back into the church.

The crows sat motionless on their Michael statue as Merrin hauled himself up the rope ladder and out of the building. The jeep was still parked in the moonlight, looking for all the world as if it sat in an ordinary parking lot. He climbed in and turned the key, half expecting that it wouldn't start. It did, and the motor's growl was a perfect slice of normality.

As Merrin drove away, he threw one last glance over his shoulder at the half-buried church. A single crow sat on the lip of the dome, outlined in the moonlight. It bobbed once, then flapped its wings and dropped back into darkness.

Merrin guided the jeep down the rutted road, his mouth set in a hard line. He arrived at the village without further incident, parked, and was heading for the hotel when he saw Emekwi sitting in the moonlight at the edge of the boardwalk, his face a mask of grief. The other man saw Merrin approach and met him halfway.

"Father Merrin," he said in a cracked and broken voice that tore Merrin's heart, "Joseph is all I have left. Please . . . you must help him."

"I'm sorry," Merrin replied. "There's nothing I can do."

Emekwi stood in Merrin's path, standing a little too close and making Merrin uncomfortable. He grabbed Merrin's hand like a supplicant. "You can pray," Emekwi said.

Fatigue pulled at Merrin, fatigue and sorrow. Emekwi was a good man, and he would have given anything to comfort the other man. But how could Merrin give someone else comfort when he could find none for himself?

"My prayers won't help, Emekwi," he said quietly. "I wish they would. Try Father Francis."

Emekwi released Merrin's hand with a sad nod. "It's the devil, Father. I fear he's come for all of us."

Merrin stared after Emekwi long after he had hurried away. Then he heard Sarah scream.

Nine

✠

Village of Derati, British East Africa

The lame know how to fall.

—Kenyan proverb

DR. SARAH NOVACK emerged from the lukewarm shower. Hot water was provided by a metal tank on the roof. It was painted black to catch as much heat from the sun as possible, and during the day the water was too hot for comfort. By this time of night—or was it morning?—the water was considerably cooler. Still, the running water relaxed her and would help her sleep. She picked up a much laundered towel, scrubbed her hair dry, and started on her body.

A scraping noise came from somewhere outside the bathroom. Sarah paused, towel in hand. Another scrape, followed by a thump. She tensed. Maybe it was just Joseph again. She doubted it.

Scrape. Thump. Thump.

Sarah wrapped the towel around herself and opened the bathroom door. A dark, empty hallway greeted her. "Hello?" she called. "Who's out there? Joseph?"

Thump.

Heart racing, she eased down the hallway in her bare feet. She stopped at her office and checked inside. Empty. She moved farther down the corridor. Kitchen and bedroom both empty.

Thump. Scrape. Thump.

Something flashed past the bedroom window. Sarah leaped back with a squeak, but whatever it was had gone.

Wrapping the towel more tightly around her breasts, she moved down to the clinic entrance and cautiously poked her head inside. The overhead lamps still burned, and Joseph lay asleep in his bed. On the table beside her, the radio exploded into static. Sarah shrieked and spun. Her foot skidded on something slippery and she almost fell down. She recovered her balance and twisted the dial to shut the radio off. How had it come on? And what had she slipped in?

Sarah looked down and saw the blood. She was standing in a puddle of it, and a crimson trail snaked down the hallway toward her. The bottom of her towel was soaked in scarlet. A tiny sound died in her throat. Her shaking hand slid down between her thighs. They came up slick and red. Sarah screamed and screamed.

Suddenly Lankester Merrin was there, and the next several moments became a blur. She was vaguely aware of Merrin moving her around, holding her up, dressing her. Her throat was sore. She felt tired. She was in a hospital bed, and Lankester was sitting next to her, wearing a serious expression.

"How do you feel?" he asked, and the sound of his voice was an amazing comfort.

"I . . . I don't know," she answered hoarsely. "What happened to me?"

"I came in and found you bleeding from the . . . well, I found you bleeding," he said. "I got you cleaned up and into a bed, then I mopped up . . . I mopped the floor."

"It's impossible," she said flatly.

"Maybe because of the stress, your body—"

"No, you don't understand." Her voice dropped to a whisper. "What the Nazis did to me . . . what they . . . there's nothing left to bleed." Memories washed up inside her, hard and painful. "It was called Chelmno."

Merrin blinked. "What was?"

"The camp," Sarah said, holding her tattoo up to the lamplight. Merrin made out B14206. "I was at Chelmno. The Nazis converted a castle and church into a work camp. They put me to work processing confiscated items."

"I don't understand," Merrin said.

"After you arrived in one of the camps, you were taken into a room where everything was taken from you. Suitcases, clothes, eyeglasses, jewelry, shoes, hair, even teeth. And your name. As you left, they gave you a number and a thin gray uniform. Once the prisoners were taken out of the room, we processors were brought in. We sorted the materials. Men's clothes into one pile, women's into another, children's into a third. Some of them were still warm from the people who wore them. I never got over finding teeth on the floor. The Nazis wanted them for the bits of gold they contained, and the guards would pull them out with pliers before sending the prisoners on to the barracks or the death chambers.

"I found family mementos in the suitcases—photographs, musical instruments, journals, and other souvenirs of the past. These people had been told they were 'relocated,' so they had taken their most valuable personal items with them. If it was paper or wood, the Nazis used it for fuel in the crematoriums. Money, gold fillings, and jewelry, of course, went to fund the army, though I know the guards stole a fair amount of it. I never learned what the Nazis did with the clothes, but we piled the shoes on the floor of the castle's church. They covered every inch of flooring so high they came up to my shins.

"I didn't spend all my time sorting possessions, of course. I saw my brother raped and my cousins shot. I saw my parents taken to the gassing vans. And yet I continued on, sorting warm piles of clothes."

Merrin studied his lap in silence. Sarah paused.

"It's this place, Lankester," she said at last. "The Turkana are right. It's cursed."

"Sarah—"

"No, there's something happening here. Something evil."

"Sarah, it's much easier to believe in evil as an entity," Merrin said. "But it's not. It's a purely human condition. Inside of us all."

"And what evil is inside you?"

"What?"

She reached out of the bed and touched the back of his hand. "I processed clothing and the past of condemned people. What happened to you?"

Silence. Sarah wondered if she should press or let it lie. More long moments of uncomfortable silence passed. Then Merrin abruptly said, "Did Bession ever talk to you about what he found under the church?"

Sarah blinked. "*Under?* No. What's under the church?"

"Another temple." Merrin gave a brief explanation, but omitted mention of the missing idol and the flies.

"No," Sarah said. "He never mentioned anything like that. It sounds horrible."

A yawn split Merrin's face in two for a moment. "Maybe I should—"

"You should go to bed," Sarah said. "I'll be fine, Lankester. You need to rest."

Merrin was too tired to argue, too tired to think about Sarah's blood, too tired to think about the flies or piles of shoes or Francis or anything else. He rose, kissed Sarah on the forehead, and left. He took the back steps through the hotel up to his room, did a perfunctory wash, and fell into bed.

What evil is inside you?

His sleep should have been deep and dreamless. Instead, Merrin tossed and turned on his thin, hard bed. The alarm clock ticked on the nightstand.

You. Priest. What is your name?

The dead Nazi lay motionless on the cobblestones in the town square. The back of his uniform shone wet with blood, and a long tear gaped in the cloth between his shoulder blades. The villagers of Hellendoorn, huddled against a stone wall in a frightened flock, eyed the body nervously. A group of Nazi soldiers stood grim guard a few paces away. They were ragged and unkempt. Some of them sported bandages, and one stood on crutches. All of them had rifles. The men, women, and children of Hellendoorn looked around in fear and trepidation, looking for some escape, finding none.

A gray drizzle fell from an equally gray sky, and everyone was soaked through. Smoke from a distant battle rose up against the low clouds. A sharp, acrid smell rode the air. Father Lankester Merrin stood near the huddle of people, his hands clasped so tightly within his black robes that his knuckles hurt.

Lieutenant Rolf Kessel stepped in front of the soldiers and began to pace. He was tall and thin, and his worn face held more wrinkles than it should have for a man his age. The twin silver lightning bolts of the SS zigzagged across his collar. Merrin bit his lower lip until he tasted blood.

"That," Kessel said without preamble, gesturing at the corpse, "was one of my men. We found him in a ditch with a kitchen knife in his back. Murdered. By one of you." He put his hands behind his back as he paced and looked up at the sky as if he expected a break in the weather. "You know the German army is retreating. It makes you feel hope. It shouldn't. We will remain here until this matter is resolved."

The villagers and Merrin remained silent.

"So," Kessel continued, "who among you is responsible?"

No answer. The villagers looked everywhere but at Kessel and his soldiers, hoping to avoid eye contact and the attention it might bring.

Kessel turned to Merrin. "You. Priest. What is your name?"

"I am Father Merrin," he said, unable to keep a quaver from his voice.

"These . . . creatures are your parish? They confess to you, then. So—point out the one who is responsible."

Merrin clenched his hands even harder. That wasn't what he had been expecting to hear. He had no idea who had killed the wretched soldier, though he did know that the man had raped at least four girls in the time he had been stationed here. Merrin didn't feel the slightest bit of sorrow over the soldier's death, though he had said a dutiful prayer when he got the news. He had followed that with a prayer of thanks. Now he was starting to regret the latter.

"No one here did this, Lieutenant," Merrin responded firmly, hoping his obvious conviction would be enough. "They aren't capable of—"

"Apparently one of them is," Kessel interrupted.

A woman in the group—Merrin recognized Marianne Wieger—began to cry. The people close by tried to hush her.

"Don't be frightened," Merrin said. "It's all right. Everything will be all right."

Kessel edged up to Merrin, who tried not to shy away.

The SS officer exuded a strange heat, and his breath smelled like fish.

"You must help me with this," he said quietly.

"What do you mean?" Merrin asked.

"I need *someone*. Do you understand? Surely there is one among them who beats his wife or his children. A thief, perhaps. Or a street beggar. Every town has someone it can do without, even a town as small as Hellendoorn. Point him out. I will take him and the matter will be resolved."

For a dreadful moment, Merrin considered doing just that. Hellendoorn did have its fair share of ne'er-do-wells. *Who would miss one or two?* whispered a little voice inside him. Then he shook his head. No one here deserved death. In any case, such things were God's province to decide, not Merrin's.

"There is no killer in that line," he said. "I know them."

Kessel studied Merrin's face. Merrin looked unflinchingly back. After a long, cold moment, Kessel seemed to find what he had been looking for.

"As you wish," he said, turning back to the villagers with a smile. "I have good news! You are all innocent. Your priest has told me so."

The villagers exchanged nervous looks. This was too easy, too good to be true. Merrin held his breath.

"The murderer is no doubt lurking in the countryside, growing brazen," Kessel said. "Perhaps brazen enough to strike at another German soldier." He paused to survey the inhabitants of Hellendoorn and their priest. "I am going to shoot ten of you, in the hope that we can demonstrate to this wretch the terrible responsibility he has incurred."

Merrin cried out as the guns began to fire. The cracks and bangs thundered against his ears . . .

. . . and merged with the sound of banging on wood.

Merrin came fully awake. The sun was well above the horizon, and someone was pounding on the door. He rolled out of bed, ignoring the way his sweaty night-clothes stuck to his body, and yanked it open.

It was Francis, fully dressed in collar and khakis. "Something's happened," he said.

Merrin pulled on some clothes, rubbed his sandy eyes, and hurried down the main stairs behind Francis. God, it was one crisis after another. He couldn't even get a full night's sleep.

"Jefferies never showed up at the dig this morning," Francis said in the main lobby. "He wasn't in his room, either. Emekwi checked, and he wasn't in his room. When they went into the bar . . ." They came to the door of the bar, and Francis pushed it open. ". . . they found this."

The place had been ransacked. Smashed tables and broken chairs littered the floor. The shelves had all been pulled down. Chuma and Emekwi stood near the door, looking grim. A cloud of flies hovered over the bar, prompting Merrin to shrink back. He noticed Francis was in no hurry to approach either, and for some reason the image of the flies crawling across his privates sprang into Merrin's mind. He pushed the image aside and forced himself to approach the bar.

Flies bounced off Merrin's head and arms, making

him shudder. A series of deep gouges marred the bar's surface—eight in all. Each had a piece of broken fingernail in it. A chill came over him.

"The chief's baby was stillborn last night," Francis said. "He blames us."

Merrin looked at him. "You think the Turkana took Jefferies out of revenge?"

"I think this place is on the verge of an uprising. I've called Major Granville. A full detachment will be here by the afternoon. They're flying in from Nairobi."

Merrin shook his head, remembering Francis's extra-heavy suitcase. *Probably had a two-way radio in it,* he thought, *no doubt supplied by the Vatican.*

"You disagree," Francis said, noticing Merrin's expression.

"It's been my experience," Merrin said, "that bringing soldiers into a situation is never a good idea."

As he turned to leave, a glint of metal caught his eye. He bent over and picked up the source. The St. Joseph medal Jefferies had given Sarah gleamed on his palm. The infant Jesus looked up at his adopted father, little knowing what awaited him in thirty years. The cross was a terrible instrument of torture, and these days Merrin found little solace in looking at it. He certainly didn't find it restful when it was used to mark graves. He shoved the medal into his pocket and strode outside into bright sunlight. Chuma followed him.

Marked graves. Like the ones just outside the village. Something nagged at him, teased at the edge of his mind. Something about the graves of those killed by the

160

plague fifty years ago. What was wrong with them? Long rows, even and neat. All of them—

All of them.

"Who buried them?" he blurted.

"Buried who?" Chuma asked.

"The people who died in the plague," Merrin clarified. "You said it killed every single person in the village fifty years ago. If that's true, who buried the bodies?"

Chuma was clearly caught off guard. "I . . . I don't know. I have never thought about it."

"Maybe it's high time we *did* think about it."

The planes landed on the salt flats near Lake Rudolf. An hour later, two military lorries rumbled into Derati. The women who were selling their wares in the center of town bundled up their blankets and rushed away, looks of fear and mistrust on their faces. No hitchhikers jumped down from these lorries. The children tried to rush around the convoy but were restrained by their parents. Merrin watched from the hotel porch.

A sergeant major with a blond crewcut jumped down from one of the lorries and ran around to undo the canvas flaps on the backs of the vehicles. Merrin grimaced and headed for the convoy. Emekwi emerged from the hotel and joined him. A group of men in red waist wraps gathered at one end of the central square.

"Where are they going to stay?" Emekwi asked. He was wary but trying to hide it. The military had a reputation for bivouacking in local hostelries without paying the bill.

"All right, come on, come on!" bellowed the sergeant major. "Out, out, out! You worthless lot of ugly bastards! First platoon on the left, second platoon on the right!"

Francis emerged from the hotel as soldiers, armed and helmeted, leaped down from the first lorry. From the second emerged Major Granville, looking travel-tired and somewhat bemused. He put on a pair of sunglasses and smiled at the group of Turkana men. They stared stony-faced in return.

"Beloved wherever we go," Granville sighed. "Sergeant Major Harris!"

"Sir!" Harris shouted instantly.

"Have the men stand at attention. I've a feeling that those gentlemen over there report to the local aristocracy, and I don't want to display even a hint of disrespect—now or at any other time. Am I clear?"

"Sir! Respect for the godforsaken fuzzies at all times, sir!"

Granville's face reddened. "Sergeant Major, that is *precisely* the sort of comment—"

"Major Granville?" interrupted Francis, trotting up to the convoy. Merrin wasn't far behind him, but was in no rush.

"Father Francis!" Granville shook Will's proffered hand. "Any answers on Jefferies?"

"I'm afraid not."

"Well, you did the right thing in calling me, Father. I've been in these situations before, and you have to stay on top of—" He suddenly paused and cocked his head, as if listening for something. Then he continued, "—on top

of these people. Trouble can spring up at a moment's—"
Again he stopped, prompting Francis to look in Merrin's direction.

"I'm not sure the Turkana are responsible for what's happening here, Major," Merrin said.

Granville, however, didn't respond. He was staring at something. Merrin followed his gaze to the door of the hotel. It yawned open like a black mouth. Emekwi emerged from it, looking uncertain.

"Major Granville?" Francis said.

Granville remembered himself, though his initial good nature seemed to be gone. "Right, right," he growled. "Responsible."

"Major, this is Emekwi," Francis said, gesturing at the man in question. "He owns the hotel."

Emekwi came forward and shook Granville's hand heartily. "My establishment shall be open to your men at all times, Major, though unfortunately I do not have enough rooms to house you all, so perhaps—"

"Nor should we accept them if you did, sir," Granville cut in. "We'll be camping near the dig." He gave the gathered elders a sidelong glance and raised his voice. "This site is too important to jeopardize. And until I'm satisfied that the excavation is secure, the British Army will assume complete control."

A hard knot contracted in Merrin's stomach. "Sir, the Turkana won't like the show of force—"

"I'm not concerned with what the Turkana like, Mr. Merrin," Granville snapped. "And if they start any more trouble, they'll have to answer to the might of His Majesty, King George."

Merrin shot Francis a *Happy now?* glance. Francis looked away.

"And what exactly *is* your mission, Major?" Merrin demanded. An hour had passed. The two military lorries were parked pointedly near the brown, blocky walls of the uncovered church, where the soldiers were already setting up camp. Shouted orders and the clank of hammers on metal stakes filled the air, overpowering the noises of the dig. A large group of red-clad Turkana warriors watched from a distant hilltop. All of them carried spears.

"Guard duty, Mr. Merrin," Granville said. "Don't worry—we won't get in the way. We only want to ensure your safety."

Merrin stared at the major, who returned his look with infuriating calm. Merrin didn't want this man here, didn't want his soldiers and their heavy boots tromping around his dig. Especially with all the strange goings-on. Granville would ask questions, questions Merrin wasn't ready to answer. The soldiers also posed a special problem. Guard duty, especially this kind of guard duty, would inevitably grow boring, and bored soldiers were dangerous. They drank and gambled and chased village women, causing no end of trouble.

The problem was, there was nothing Merrin could do about it. Granville was in charge of the Turkana district, a baron in his own little fiefdom. And Merrin wasn't even technically in charge of the dig. Will Francis was. If Granville decided to blast the church out of the ground with dynamite, it would be done. Merrin would have to walk carefully.

He shot a glance at the hilltop and noticed that the warriors were gone. In the distance, a plume of smoke curled up to the sky. Merrin excused himself to the major and hurried toward the smoke. He arrived at a point halfway between the village and the dig site. At the base of a rocky hillside gathered a crowd of villagers, all clad in their finest, brightest clothes. It looked as if a rainbow had shattered on the stones. An impressive pile of wood lay in the center of the crowd, and it had just been set alight. A small, sad bundle wrapped in white lay in Lokiria's arms. Sebituana stood next to her, his face devoid of emotion.

As Merrin approached, three of the village men struck a rhythm on their drums and two others wailed a sad melody on a pair of wooden flutes. Chuma, standing at the edge of the crowd, saw Merrin and hurried over.

"You shouldn't be here," Chuma said.

Merrin didn't stop, or even slow down. His presence spread through the Turkana like an angry wave. Several warriors came forward to block his path, with Jomo in the forefront. The men glared at Merrin with loathing as palpable as the flames that licked the pyre. Merrin nodded to them as if they had met while passing on the street. The drumming stopped in mid-beat.

"Please tell Sebituana that I'm sorry for his loss," Merrin said.

"You are not welcome here," Jomo said in words brittle and sharp as broken glass.

"I need to know about the plague that destroyed this village."

"It wasn't a plague," Jomo replied.

The reply surprised Merrin. "Then what was it?"

"The evil inside your church." Jomo's tone made it clear he thought Merrin the worst kind of fool. "It's taken Emekwi's elder son. And it's only getting stronger. You must abandon your work, or we will be forced to stop you."

The crowd rippled at this. Every eye was on Merrin, who suddenly felt vulnerable and alone. Never had he felt such anger and hatred directed at him. The warriors tensed like lions ready to spring. Their spears looked sharp enough to pierce flesh and bone with agonizing ease. The fire crackled and snapped. Chuma tugged on Merrin's sleeve, urging him to leave. Quickly.

Merrin stood his ground. "So you won't tell me what happened here fifty years ago?"

Jomo's response came in Turkana, and the words made Chuma blanch. Jomo, Sebituana, and the other warriors turned their backs and gathered around the fire once more. The drums began again, but none of the tension left the air.

"What did he say?" Merrin demanded.

Chuma hesitated, and Merrin wanted to shake the answer from him. At last, Chuma said, "He doesn't need to tell you because it's happening again. Right now."

Sebituana stepped toward the fire, took the little bundle from his wife, and carefully laid it among the flames. The wrappings caught fire and the body began to burn. A lump came to Merrin's throat. It was so sad and unfair for parents to build a funeral pyre for a . . . for a . . .

He whirled on Chuma. "You don't bury your dead here in Derati. You cremate them."

"Yes," Chuma said, not sure what Merrin was on about now.

"Then who the hell is buried in that graveyard?"

Ten

✝

Catholic cemetery, British East Africa

We must add wisdom to knowledge.

—Kenyan proverb

THE SUN TOUCHED THE HORIZON, but Merrin kept digging. His shovel bit into the sandy earth in front of the white stone cross. Sweat prickled on his back, arms, and neck. His muscles burned. The jeep was parked behind him at the edge of the graveyard like a patient dog waiting by itself. Merrin had tried to get help in the endeavor, but none of the villagers would go near the cemetery, no matter how much he offered in payment. And in the end he had realized that digging a grave was a one-man job.

Pausing to dash sweat from his forehead, he caught sight of something moving, a silhouette against the red setting sun. It carried a spear. Jomo? Merrin shaded his eyes for a better look, but the figure was gone. He looked back down at the hole he had begun over the grave. Maybe he was being foolish. Maybe he'd been reading too much into the story about the plague. Plagues never killed *everyone*. There were always a few survivors. Though would an especially virulent plague leave enough people behind to bury all the dead? The Black Death in Europe certainly hadn't. Was he desecrating this place? He hadn't asked for permission to exhume anything. That said, who was he supposed to ask?

Merrin took a slug of water from his canteen, rolled up his sleeves, and went back to work. There was a rhythm to it. Shove the shovel into the ground, press it down with his foot, heave the dirt up and out. Shove, press, heave. Shove, press, heave. He was going to have blisters for this, even with the gloves, but still he kept on. Shove, press, heave. Shove, press, heave.

The sun slipped away, leaving dark pools of shadow behind. Merrin paused long enough to light a kerosene lamp and went back to work. Shove, press, heave. He tried not to think about how eerie it was to be digging in a graveyard by lamplight after dark. Childhood stories of vampires and zombies slithered through his mind, giving the night glittering teeth and clicking claws as it gathered in around him. Shove, press, heave. Shove, press, heave. He was two feet down, then three.

A cold, inhuman laugh in his ear made his scalp prickle. He spun around, waist deep in the earth. Three hyenas were standing at the edge of the grave, so close he could feel their breath as they panted on his bare arms. Their eyes, glowing red in the lamplight, looked straight into Merrin's own. A drop of saliva slid down one hyena's fang and landed on the sandy soil. Merrin heard it hit, a tiny *thip* sound. He didn't move. Couldn't move.

The lead hyena exhaled hard. Its breath was cold and stank of gangrene. Merrin braced himself for pain—

—and then the hyenas were gone, vanished into the darkness. Merrin became aware that both his hands were in pain. He looked down and saw his gloved fingers clenched so tightly around the handle of the shovel they were probably leaving grooves. Forcing himself to relax his grip, he sagged against the side of the grave, panting with the aftermath. Hyena tracks pitted the dust all around. He should go back to the village. The danger after dark was all too clear. But it felt like the hyenas didn't *want* Merrin to finish digging up the grave, as if they wanted to stop him, to control him. Just like the Church wanted to do.

Merrin frowned with resolve and went back to digging. Shove, press, heave. Shove, press, heave. The sound was as rhythmic as a drum, or marching footsteps. Shove, press, heave. Shove, press, tromp. Tromp, press, tromp. The sounds of digging became like jackboots stomping across cobblestones, the same cobblestones Merrin had walked back in Hellendoorn. He tried to push the image away, but it only came back stronger.

You. Priest. What is your name?

"Shut up," Merrin snarled.

They confess to you, then. So—point out the one who is responsible.

"I said, shut up!" The shovel kept moving, but the memory wouldn't go away.

I need someone. Do you understand? Surely there is one who beats his wife or his children. A thief, perhaps. Or a street beggar. Every town has someone it can do without, even a town as small as Hellendoorn. Point him out. I will take him and the matter will be resolved.

"There is no killer in that line," Merrin said through clenched teeth and closed eyes. "I know them."

"The murderer is no doubt lurking in the countryside, growing brazen," Kessel said. "Perhaps brazen enough to strike at another German soldier." He paused to survey the inhabitants of Hellendoorn and their priest. "I am going to shoot ten of you, in the hope that we can demonstrate to this wretch the terrible responsibility he has incurred."

A jolt thundered through the villagers. They stared at each other, then at Merrin, in terror and disbelief. Merrin's heart jerked sideways. The thin, cold rain continued to fall, soaking the villagers and the cold corpse of the Nazi soldier. The corpse had a long, bloody knife wound in the back, and its eyes were open. Kessel scanned the crowd and settled on a man in his thirties. Nico Tuur. Kessel drew his pistol, yanked Nico from the crowd, and forced him to his knees on the street. The other soldiers aimed their weapons at the remaining villagers.

God, please tell me what to do, Merrin thought desperately, hands folded inside his black robe. *Help this loyal servant.*

"You have big hands," Kessel said, putting the barrel

of his pistol to Nico's temple. Nico swallowed visibly. "I think you are a farmer. Do you have children?"

"Yes," Nico whispered. "Two girls."

Please, Lord . . .

"Excellent. We'll start with you." Kessel released the safety.

"Stop!" Merrin shouted.

The lieutenant turned without moving his gun. "You have some objection, priest?"

"In God's name, you cannot do this!"

"I do nothing in God's name, priest. But of course, you are right." Kessel holstered his pistol and kicked Nico back into the group of villagers. "I think it would be best for *you* to choose the ten."

Merrin stared. "What?"

"They're your flock. You live among them. I'm only passing through. So you choose ten to die." Kessel stretched his lips over yellowed teeth. "In God's name."

"I—" Merrin swallowed. "I will not."

"Give me ten of them or I will kill them all. Men, women, and children."

There was only one way out that Merrin could see. Terror clawed at his chest. Praying with every fiber of his being, he forced himself to move between Kessel and the villagers in the cold, drizzly rain. *Our Father who art in Heaven . . .*

"*I* killed your man," he said. "One of the girls he raped told me what happened. I . . . I lost my temper and grabbed a knife. When I found him in the village, I stabbed him in the back and left him. The blame is mine. Shoot me."

There was a long pause. Kessel looked at Merrin, at the villagers, and at the corpse. Merrin stood his ground, though his bladder felt heavy and his hands shook. *Will someone be able to administer last rites?* he wondered as he met Kessel's harsh gaze.

At last Kessel said, "Liar. But I understand. The good shepherd offers to die so that his sheep may live. I think not. I will shoot ten, priest. And you will choose them. You have five seconds."

"I . . . can't," Merrin whispered.

Kessel reached out and grabbed the nearest person to him, a teenaged girl named Aartje Kroon. He brought the pistol up. Before Merrin could react, Kessel pressed the barrel to her temple and fired.

The sound of the shot was horrible. Blood spattered the horrified villagers, and Aartje's body slumped bonelessly to the ground. Her ruined head hit the cobblestones with a sickening crack. Merrin stared down at her, stunned and speechless.

"Now choose!" Kessel shouted. "Choose ten more, or I will shoot them all."

Merrin was still unable to speak. Blood snaked red over the stones. Aartje's parents screamed uncontrollably, trying to get to her body, but the others held them back. Merrin saw the pleading in the eyes of the villagers, the hope that he would find some way out of this. His mind raced in a dozen different directions, but nothing came to him. No thoughts, no ideas. Nothing. In the end, he did the only thing he could do: he bowed his head and clasped his hands.

Hear me, O Lord, he thought. *Tell me what to do.*

Help me save these good people. Don't let Your servants be murdered like this.

"What?" Kessel demanded. "Are you praying? To God?" He leaned closer, and Merrin could smell the fish on his breath again. "Then pray, Father. Because I know something, you see."

Kessel grabbed young Martin Greter, who had celebrated his ninth birthday only yesterday. He shoved the barrel of his pistol into the boy's face. Martin's eyes went wide.

"Please!" his mother cried. "Oh God!"

"I know that God is not here today, priest," Kessel finished.

Hear me, O Lord . . .

Kessel's finger tightened on the trigger. Still Merrin could not speak. Abruptly the lieutenant frowned and shoved Martin back into the crowd. His mother snatched him weeping into her arms. Kessel faced Merrin.

"You win, priest," he said, then shouted to his men, "Shoot them all!"

With a snap, the soldiers brought their rifles up. The villagers screamed and wailed against the wall.

"Wait!" Merrin shouted.

The soldiers paused. Kessel looked at Merrin expectantly. The street fell absolutely silent.

Hear me . . . hear me, O . . . O Lord . . .

Nothing came to him. No ideas. No words. No alternatives. Save one.

Hands shaking like leaves in a storm, Merrin raised an arm to point. "Joost Harmensz."

Joost looked at him in shock. Merrin's throat closed.

One of the soldiers stepped forward to pull the man from the crowd, but Kessel halted him with a gesture.

"Too late, Father," he said. "You had your chance. Kill them all!"

Inside Merrin something broke. He flung himself down in front of Kessel, his wet robe flapping like heavy wings. "No!" he begged. "Please! Take Joost! And him— Klaus Briejer. And Erica van Hout!"

A cold wind whirled up the street, scattering droplets and rustling Merrin's black robes. Kessel smiled down at him. "Good, Father. Good."

Soldiers dragged the people Merrin had indicated from the ranks of the villagers and forced them to their knees in a line. Three shots cracked through the air and they fell to the ground.

"Seven more," Kessel said with a smile. "Who shall be next?"

And Father Lankester Merrin raised his arm to point.

Sarah sat upright in bed. Footsteps and low voices were coming from the clinic. She yanked on some clothes, dashed down the hallway, and stopped dead in the clinic doorway. A crowd of ghosts, white and spectral, surrounded Joseph's bed. Then she caught sight of Emekwi standing among them, and the scene snapped into clearer focus. She was looking at four Turkana warriors, dressed in nothing but loincloths, their bodies covered in white clay. A fifth Turkana, older than the rest, carried a covered basket and a rattle made of antelope hooves tied loosely together at the end of a heavy stick. The warriors were tying Joseph's wrists and ankles to the bed. The older man—clearly a shaman—shook the rattle over Joseph, who was staring upward, his eyes vague and cloudy. Weepy lesions covered the boy's face and neck. Tears ran down Emekwi's face.

"I'm sorry," he said softly.

"What are you doing?" Sarah demanded. "That's my patient!"

The men ignored her. The shaman set the rattle down and drew a wicked-looking knife from the basket.

"No!" Sarah screamed, and charged. Two sets of rough hands grabbed her up and hoisted her away, kicking and snarling. For a horrible moment, Sarah was back in the camp at Chelmno, with the guards snatching at her, tossing her around like a broken toy. She twisted and spat and fought with hysterical strength, but the guards—the warriors—were stronger. The shaman raised the knife over Joseph's chest. The boy began to shudder and shake. The hanging lamps dimmed and their chimneys rattled. The shaman's knife flicked downward.

"No!" Sarah screamed again. But the shaman only slashed open Joseph's pajamas, leaving behind a long, thin cut on the boy's chest. It oozed blood. The shaman set the knife aside and took a clay jar from the basket. Using wooden tongs, he plucked several small black objects from the jar and laid them along the cut on Joseph's chest.

Sarah realized they were leeches. They clamped down on Joseph's skin. She swore she could hear sucking sounds. Sarah lost what little composure she had left, and with a shriek of fear and rage, she fought against the warriors holding her back. Then she felt cold metal at her neck. One of the warriors held a knife against her throat, the threat clear even without words. Sarah went absolutely still. The shaman picked up the knife and rattle again.

Emekwi abruptly bolted for the door, his face twisted with conflicting emotions. He fled into the night with a choked sob. Sarah, still held captive by the knife, had no such choice. She watched in cold horror as the shaman began a low chant. He rattled the antelope hooves over Joseph with one hand and raised the knife with the other.

Will Francis wandered aimlessly about Derati, heading more or less in the direction of the hospital. Maybe he'd drop in on Dr. Novack for a little conversation.

He rounded the corner just in time to see Emekwi flee the hospital, a horror-stricken look on his face. The man was clearly in horrible distress. What on earth . . . ?

"Emekwi?" Will said.

"I didn't know what else to do," Emekwi said hoarsely. "Forgive me." He was gone before Will could respond. Then he heard screams from the hospital.

Sarah could see that the shaman's next blow was intended to go straight to Joseph's heart. His convulsions shook the bed. The lamp flames danced and flickered madly. One of the warriors grabbed Joseph's arm in an attempt to hold him still.

Snap.

The warrior holding Joseph looked down in confu-

178

sion, then shock and pain. His index finger had bent backward until the bone had broken. Even as he stared at his hand, his middle finger twitched. The warrior's breathing grew rapid as he tried to fight whatever force was working on his hand. His fourth and fifth fingers began to bend as well. Sarah watched in horrified fascination as the fingers bent inexorably backward. The warrior screamed.

Snap snap snap.

The shaman shouted something in Turkana and brought the knife down. The bones in his wrist and forearm shattered and his arm twisted sideways at a gruesome angle. The knife clattered to the floor.

Sarah was vaguely aware of Father Francis bursting into the room as the place erupted into mayhem. The injured warrior and the shaman howled in agony. The left leg of another warrior bent backward at the knee and shattered with a hideous wet splintering noise. Overhead the lamps flickered like strobe lights, making shadows dance and gibber in the corners.

Snap snap snap.

Sarah lost track of whose bones bent and broke. The warriors and the shaman scrambled away from the bed, helping their more injured compatriots, all of whom were screaming. Sarah was flung to the ground. Blood ran from their wounds, and Sarah caught glimpses of yellow-white bone. The bed shook and pounded against the floor. Francis tried to reach the bed, but was knocked back by an unseen force. He slammed into the wall. The warriors and the shaman got to the front door and fled into the night.

Instantly the room went still. The bed stopped moving, and the kerosene lamps cast a serene yellow glow. Silence rang through the room. Sarah pushed herself upright, then staggered to her feet. Father Francis pulled himself to a standing position. A bruise was already forming on his cheek. Sarah stumbled over to the bed and fumbled with the ropes that restrained Joseph's hands. His lesions leaked thick, bubbly fluid. Francis ran over and grabbed her wrist.

"Don't!" he cried.

"Get off me!" Sarah shoved him away, but he came right back.

"Sarah, no!" He grabbed her wrist again, and she fought back, this time with more success. Francis didn't retreat. "Sarah, stop! The boy's dangerous! Didn't you see?"

"I don't know what I saw," Sarah said stubbornly.

"Yes, you do," he insisted. "He crippled all those men. Could a *child* have done that? Could anything human have done that? The devil's responsible, Sarah. He's possessed Joseph."

His words made Sarah laugh, though the sound came out edged and harsh. "Possession? No. There must be another . . . another explanation for . . ."

She couldn't finish the sentence. Her head was filled instead with images of bending fingers and breaking bone, of bloody trails and shaking beds. It was ridiculous! Stories of demonic possession were just that—stories. No one seriously believed in such things. Freud and those who came after him had proven that simple hysteria was the root cause of so-called curses and possessions. Sarah's unexpected bleeding could probably be traced to some sort of post-stress reaction. Again—hysteria.

Except hysteria wouldn't cause bone to bend and break. Hysteria wouldn't cause the lights to flicker or the bed to jump. Hysteria wouldn't cause the hyenas to ignore Joseph while they devoured James.

"He needs an exorcism, Sarah," Francis said. "To cast out the devil with the power of God."

"Then why don't you do one?" Sarah asked. Her tone was snide, but she couldn't seem to help herself. The scientist in her was still trying to wrap itself around this both obvious and ridiculous idea.

"Because I can't do it alone," Francis replied.

"Get Lankester, then."

"He's too far from God. He won't listen."

" 'He' who? Lankester or God?"

Francis didn't answer.

"Dammit, Francis," Sarah snarled, "what happened to him in the War?"

The door slammed open. Sarah jumped, expecting more warriors or strange phenomena. But it was Lankester Merrin, disheveled and sweaty and covered with dirt. Behind him outside, the sky was lightening with the dawn.

"They're empty!" he growled.

"What—?" Francis said.

Before Sarah or Francis could react, Merrin charged across the room, grabbed Francis by the shirt, and shoved him through the doorway, hard. Francis stumbled outside, grunting in surprise. Merrin followed, grabbed him again, and shoved him against the wall. Sarah rushed outside, face pale.

"I dug up three graves, and the coffins were all empty!" Merrin pulled Francis forward and slammed him against the wall again.

"Lankester, no!" Sarah shouted. "What are you doing?"

Merrin didn't listen. "What happened here?" he hissed through clenched teeth.

Francis strained to get his bearings. "I don't know—"

Merrin slammed him a second time. "Yes, you *do!* You've been lying to me since we got here!"

"Let go of me," Francis said, rallying.

A third slam. This time the priest's head cracked against the wood and he groaned in pain. "Don't keep up the charade, you bastard! It's all a farce. The Turkana burn their dead, but there are crosses on the graves—on the coffins. That means the Church buried them, didn't it? *Didn't it?*" He gave Francis a shake.

"Lankester—" Sarah began again.

"Yes," Francis said.

"What?" Sarah said.

"Yes," Francis repeated. "It's true. The Church ordered empty coffins to be buried in false graves."

Merrin didn't let go. "Why? What were they hiding?"

"That this place is damned," Francis said simply.

"Don't give me that," Merrin barked. "It's a line of—"

"No!" Francis interrupted sharply. "You asked the question, you're going to listen to the answer. There was a massacre here. Fifteen hundred years ago. A Byzantine army led by two priests was searching for the source of a powerful evil. They found it here, in this place. They tried to fight it, contain it, but the evil devoured them, twisting their thoughts. They enslaved the natives and forced them to build the lower temple, and there they performed blood rites and sacrifices. The Byzantines thought they were imprisoning the evil, but they were feeding it instead. Eventually the priests, natives, and soldiers turned against each other in a fury of blood that only a single priest survived. When he heard of the carnage, Emperor Justinian ordered a new church built over the site, then buried in order to seal the evil inside. All mention of it was to be stricken from the history texts forever."

"But it wasn't," Merrin stated.

"No," Francis said. "Fifty years ago, a Vatican researcher found an ancient letter in the archives. Four priests came to examine the site, enlisting the people of this valley in their search. And they all disappeared."

"Where did they go?" Sarah asked, not sure if she felt more fascinated than ill.

"No one knows. The Vatican ordered a cover-up. The false graveyard. The tale of a plague to scare people away."

"But then there was the gold rush, which brought people back. And then the British stumbled across the church," Merrin said. Sarah noticed he hadn't relaxed his grip on Francis.

"Yes. And I was sent here to see if the legend was . . . real."

"What legend?" Merrin's teeth were clenched again.

"That after the war in heaven . . ." Francis's voice

trailed to a whisper. ". . . *this* is the place where Lucifer fell to earth."

A pause, and Merrin released Francis so abruptly that the other man lost his balance for a moment. Merrin turned his face away and made a strangled sound. Sarah couldn't tell if it was a laugh or a cry. In his bed, Joseph stared emptily at the ceiling.

Francis put a hand on Merrin's shoulder. "God brought you here, Lankester," he said.

Merrin shook him off. "Leave me alone."

"No. The devil is *here*," Francis insisted. "Inside that boy. The Turkana know it. They came to drive the devil from him, and he almost killed them. You can't run from this. You must help me."

"I can't," Merrin said in a broken voice.

"But surely you have to believe—"

Merrin rounded on him. "I believe in *nothing*."

The two men stared at each other for a long moment. At last Francis gave a sad and heavy sigh. "Then I have no more use for you," he said, and went back inside the hospital.

Sarah shot a glance at Merrin, but he didn't meet her eyes and looked away instead. Deafening silence gave way to the sound of an engine. Chuma pulled up to them in his jeep.

"They've found Jefferies," he said.

Eleven

✠

Archaeological survey site, British East Africa

The cruel people are consumed on the celebration day.

—Kenyan proverb

THE SUN WAS AT ITS STRONGEST by the time Merrin and Chuma reached the dig site. Soldiers swarmed over the place like army ants. They had apparently dug through the night and cleared the area around the church's main doors. The archaeologist in Merrin was furious—who knew how much information they had destroyed with their picks and shovels? Leaping from the jeep the moment Chuma braked, he sprinted over the rocky ground toward the newly uncovered building. Someone had poured a liquid—mineral oil?—on the stone hinges, and Major Granville himself was thrusting an enormous crowbar into the crack between the great

185

doors. A contingent of soldiers stood nearby, looking angry and alert.

"Major!" Merrin shouted. "Wait!"

"I will do no such thing," Granville snapped, and heaved on the bar. He encountered a moment of resistance, then the doors groaned open.

A cloud of flies boiled out of the church. Merrin and the others shielded their faces, and the insects buzzed angrily before dispersing in the light breeze. Granville started inside, but Merrin seized his arm.

"What's going on, Major?" Merrin demanded.

"One of my men took a little climb down your rope ladder last night on a dare, Mr. Merrin," Granville said. "He told me what he found."

"Why didn't anyone notify me?"

"We couldn't find you, Mr. Merrin," Granville said. He wrenched his arm from Merrin's grip and strode into the church.

Daylight flooded the building from the open doors. More flies gathered in a buzzing chorus. A terrible stench made Merrin gag. He followed the major deeper into the church, the soldiers right behind him. Granville got midway up the main aisle and sucked in a great breath. Merrin halted and stared.

Caught in the spotlight of the open dome was the corpse of Trenton Jefferies. It was strung up between Michael statues like a gory ornament on a line of Christmas tinsel. At first glance Jefferies appeared to have wings of his own, but Merrin saw the skin of the man's back had been flayed and peeled outward to create the effect. He also looked to have a white tail. It was his broken spine, dangling between his legs. Bits of rib still poked out from it. Jefferies's face was a cratered ruin.

Granville staggered backward. A soldier threw up, and Merrin's own gorge rose. He swallowed hard.

"Mother of God," Granville whispered. Then he recovered himself. "Get him down!"

None of the soldiers moved, except the one who was retching. They were frozen by the sight.

"*Get him down!*" the major barked, and this time the soldiers moved. Their efforts were hampered when they discovered the material that held Jefferies strung between the statues was a long loop of his own bowel. The skin wings collapsed into a sloppy pile.

Granville's head jerked around. "What was that?"

"What was what?" Merrin asked.

"I thought I heard— There it is again."

Merrin listened. The only sound was the muted conversation of the soldiers and the wet rustling noises they created in cutting down Jefferies's corpse. "Major—"

Granville's head jerked around again. His breathing came quick and shallow. He reached out a shaking hand into the shadows, as if he were straining to touch something. Concerned, Merrin stepped closer to him.

"Major, are you—"

Granville snapped to himself. His breathing returned to normal and his hand stopped shaking. "Savages," he whispered. "Bloody savages."

"Sorry?" Merrin said, but Granville was already striding out of the church and into the hot, harsh sunlight. Merrin looked around the church again, trying to understand what had just happened. Who had brought Jefferies down here and done this to him? And why? Jefferies was far from the best of men, but even he didn't deserve this kind of treatment.

Then the meaning behind Granville's comment penetrated Merrin's mind. He spun and ran from the church. Outside he found Granville a short distance from the site. He was striding toward a group of Turkana with a hurried, unsteady gait. Jomo, spear in hand, moved to the front of the group as the major stopped in front of him.

"Savages," Granville repeated with rising intensity. "Bloody savages!"

"Major!" Merrin shouted, still running. "No!"

Before anyone could react further, Granville yanked his sidearm from its holster and shot the warrior leader in the face. The bullet exploded out the back of his head and sprayed the men behind him with blood. Jomo dropped like a butchered bull. Merrin was only aware that he was running and screaming at the same time with a troop of soldiers right behind him. Granville was moving away, waving his pistol. Two opportunistic flies had already alighted on the steaming ruin of Jomo's head.

The initial shock passed, and the warriors howled their anger to the sky. They pressed forward. The soldiers, shocked themselves, raised their rifles and shouted at the Turkana to keep back. The warriors hesitated. Rifles clacked. Tension rode heavy in the air. Merrin started toward Jomo's body, but Chuma appeared and cut him off.

"You must go," he urged hoarsely. "Quickly! They believe the evil is upon us, that it's inside Joseph. They're going to kill him."

A Turkana raised his spear to the hot heavens and let loose a war cry. Others around him took up the sound. The cry thirsted for justice, screamed for revenge. It didn't care if it lived or died in the pursuit as long as it took everyone else with it. It chilled Merrin's blood.

"Go!" Chuma repeated, and gave Merrin a rough shove. Merrin ran. Behind him he heard a shot. He glanced over his shoulder and saw a warrior go down as the Turkana surged toward the soldiers. Chuma was nowhere to be seen. A warrior hurled his spear and skewered a soldier through the neck. The man clawed at the shaft sticking out of his throat before dropping to the bloody dust. Merrin reached his jeep and roared away with the sound of gunfire in his ears.

He drove down the rutted road as fast as he dared until he came to the village. British soldiers dashed in every direction, rifles and pistols at the ready. Drums throbbed in the distance, mingling with rifle fire. Merrin rushed into the clinic, his heart in his mouth, and found Father Francis kneeling in prayer next to Joseph's bed. The boy was shaking like a leaf in a thunderstorm. A low, animal growl issued from his throat.

"Where's Sarah?" Merrin asked breathlessly.

Francis didn't open his eyes or change position. "I don't know."

"You must leave. Now!"

"Why?"

Merrin ignored the question. In a swift move, he gathered up Joseph—the boy was surprisingly heavy—and ran from the clinic. Francis scrambled to follow and caught up as Merrin was placing Joseph in the back of the jeep.

"Take him to Father Gionetti in Nairobi," Merrin instructed. "He'll be able to . . ." He trailed off, his eyes on the distant horizon beyond the village.

"Able to what?" Francis said, then followed Merrin's gaze. The sky beyond the village was obsured by a black curtain, accompanied by the faint sound of howling wind.

"What is that?" Francis asked.

"Sandstorm," Merrin said.

"It won't let us leave," Francis murmured in awe.

The drums grew louder, pounding at Merrin's bones. A gunshot sliced the air, followed by a scream.

"We have to hide him, Francis," Merrin said with a gesture toward Joseph. The boy's eyes were open, but staring at nothing. "The Turkana are coming."

"The church?" Francis suggested.

"No. Jefferies was murdered there, and his corpse was mangled. Granville figured the Turkana did it, and he shot Jomo. Now both sides are on the warpath. The dig site is too dangerous."

"Joseph's people won't go in there. It's his only chance. There's a back way to get there—rougher, but the Turkana won't think we'd use it."

Francis jumped into the jeep and cranked it to life. Merrin wanted to stop him, tell him it wouldn't work, but he couldn't think of any other option. Francis put the jeep in gear. There was fear in his eyes, but also determination. "Aren't you coming?"

Merrin shook his head. "I have to find Sarah. We'll meet you. Take this." From his pocket he pulled *The Book of Roman Rituals*. He'd been carrying it with him ever since meeting Father Gionetti in Nairobi, though he wasn't sure why. His eyes met Francis's for a long moment. Then Francis accepted the book with a nod.

"And *you* had better take this," he said, and pressed a small object into Merrin's hand. It was a bottle of holy water. "You might need it. I have a spare."

Merrin shoved the bottle into his pocket. It clinked against the St. Joseph medal he had found in the bar, the medal Jefferies had given to Sarah. Before Merrin could respond further, Will Francis drove away.

The rising wind made the tent flap and shudder. War drums beat, sounding close by, then far off as the wind shifted and changed. The rifle fire had died down. Major Dennis Granville sat at his camp desk, watching a butterfly struggle to get out of its jar. An ether-soaked cotton ball sat beside it. Four of Granville's men were dead, pinned to the ground by Turkana spears just like his butterflies were pinned to the mounting board. He neither knew nor cared how many Turkana had died before the bloody savages had retreated to the hills. Corporal Finn would take care of the paperwork, leaving the major himself free to tend his collection. He took it with him wherever he went, the wood and glass display cases packed in crates stuffed with raw wool, and the first thing he did whenever he arrived somewhere was unpack them for display in his quarters—or in this case, his tent. Besides being nice to look at, the butterflies were neat and tidy, perfectly arranged on mounting board where they could be properly appreciated instead of fluttering messily through the forest where birds could eat them or animals might tread on them.

Granville liked order. He felt it his duty to impose tidiness and precision wherever he might be, whether it was by seeing his commands carried out or by bringing proper civilization to the jungle savages.

The butterfly had stopped moving. Granville unscrewed the jar, releasing a puff of ether, and teased the butterfly onto a mounting board. The mounting board was made of balsa wood, soft enough to stick pins into, and it had a groove down the center. Granville used a pair of tweezers to twitch the butterfly into place, so that its body lay in the board's groove. The butterfly itself was a gold-banded forester, with shimmering purple wings tipped with wide black and yellow stripes. A perfect specimen. As Granville reached for the box of pins, the tent flap opened. Corporal Finn stepped in and saluted.

"Sir," he said, "the Turkana are preparing to attack."

Granville selected the pins he would need—a number three and several double-oughts. Sometimes the world resisted order. Sometimes it fought back against the rightful order Granville tried to impose. The lazy natives didn't appreciate working in gold mines for a decent English wage. The blasted Catholics put their noses into military business. The savage Turkana murdered good white men.

The image of Jefferies's flayed corpse among the Michaels rose up in his mind. Granville set his jaw. His men would take care of that. In the meantime, he could impose a little more order on the universe right here, right now.

"Sir," Finn said again. "The—"

"Leave me," Granville said, irritated.

Finn hesitated. "Sir, I—"

"Leave!" Granville thundered. His breath made the butterfly's wings flap. Finn vanished from the tent. With rock-steady hands, Granville held a number-three pin above the gold-banded forester's thorax, just a little to the right of the mid-line. A fluttering sound brushed his hearing. He turned his head, seeking the source. He saw nothing. Odd. He checked the position of the pin again and pierced the butterfly's body, driving the pin into the balsa wood. Perfect. Next he covered the butterfly's left wings with a sheet of clear glassine paper. Gunshots cracked in the distance, but Granville ignored them. With precise, practiced movements, he pierced the glassine and pinned the butterfly's wings flat with the double-ought pins. Neat and orderly. By the time he had this specimen properly mounted, his men would no doubt have taken care of those godless savages. They would lay the bodies in neat, tidy rows for his inspection. The major set another sheet of glassine over the butterfly's right wings and pinned those down as well. After two or three days, he would remove the glassine and all the pins except the center one, pin a label to the board—*Euphaedra neophron*—and put the butterfly in a display case like the others.

The fluttering sound returned. Granville looked around again, but still saw nothing. It must be stress. He wiped a hand across his forehead, then looked down at the butterfly again in satisfaction of a job well done. There was something wet on his forehead where his fingers had touched. Granville checked his hands.

They were covered with blood. Granville gasped and his eyes went wide. Scarlet dripped onto the mounting board, which no longer held a butterfly. Granville stared down at the crow, its black and bloody feathers spread and pinned down. It was twitching. A tiny gasping sound emerged from its yellow beak, and the eye that looked up at Granville was bright with pain. The fluttering sound grew louder. Granville looked around, searching for the source, and finally found it. The glass-front cases that lined the floor of his tent were full of fluttering butterflies. Their wings moved madly, as if they were angels pinned by spears. Granville heard the tiny squeaks, the soft, insistent rustling sound. The noise grew louder, accusatory. It whispered to him, whispered that he was ineffective, worthless, powerless. No matter how many orders he gave, no matter how many plans he devised, the world would devolve into unpredictable chaos.

Tiny black legs thrashed, antennae waved. Granville felt the chaos wash around him, and the events of the day came crashing down on him. Jefferies's horrifying corpse. The confrontation with the Turkana. The ruined, mushy face of the warrior he had shot. There was no order, no order at all. He was a worthless smear of a man, not fit for the uniform he wore.

The butterflies squirmed and flapped. One of the cases actually bumped against its neighbor. The crow stiffened and went still. Its bowels let go, flooding the board with foul liquid. Granville pulled his service revolver from its holster. It felt heavy and comforting. He pressed the barrel against his temple to see what it felt like.

The butterflies stopped moving. Granville held his breath, but they remained perfectly still. With a slow hand, he lowered the gun.

Something squirmed inside his mouth.

One single black leg, then a second pushed out from between his lips. Granville made a choking noise, and a purple butterfly with yellow and black markings on its wings crawled from his mouth as if it were emerging from its cocoon. It crawled across his cheeks, flapping its wings to dry them. Granville felt its tiny feet tickling his skin, felt like he was falling into a deep, black pit.

In one swift motion, he shoved the gun into his mouth and fired.

Sand whirled on the wind, giving it claws and teeth. Merrin shoved open the door to the clinic and ran through it to the back, passing a full-length mirror in the hallway. Behind Merrin's back, a pale, fanged face appeared in the glass, soft as a nightmare. He burst into Sarah's kitchen, shouting her name, but she wasn't there. An icicle of fear stabbed his heart. Had the Turkana already—?

No, she was fine. She would be here somewhere. He

hurried back up the hallway, passed the mirror again, and paused. Someone was staring at him. He could feel cold eyes on the back of his neck. Merrin whirled, and the mirror shattered into silver shards. Outside, the wind continued to prowl around the building, scratching at windows and scrabbling at doors.

Merrin left the broken mirror to check the tiny sitting room, then the bathroom. "Sarah!" No answer. He dashed over to her bedroom. Faint light leaked from under the door. Merrin reached for the knob, then froze as a shadow passed in front of the light. A floorboard creaked inside the room. If it was Sarah, why hadn't she answered? Rustling sounds skittered beyond the door. Merrin braced himself and burst inside.

Chaos filled the room. Clothes, books, and tarot cards lay strewn everywhere. The window was broken, and the wind whistled through torn mosquito netting. Flies buzzed and swarmed. Something had clawed the mattress to shreds. The stench of a sewer pervaded the air. On one wall was a finger-painting of the statue Merrin had seen under the church—a man with wings and a lion's head, with a serpent where the penis should be. In the center of the painting's chest, rammed straight into the plaster, was the blocky idol from Semelier's rubbing, the one missing from the statue under the church. Flies swarmed over the painting in a happy orgy. Merrin looked closer, gagging as he realized the work had been done in blood and feces. Where was Sarah? Was that *her* blood?

He forced himself to set his hands on the idol and, ignoring the flies that crawled down his arms, pulled it from the wall. It was heavy and solid. He set it on the torn mattress for a better look. Broken springs creaked.

A photograph lay among the tarot cards scattered on the bed. Merrin picked it up. It was a wedding picture framed in silver. Half the glass was shattered, and all Merrin could make out beneath the haze of cracks was Sarah, dressed in a lacy white gown. She was smiling becomingly at the camera. Merrin picked the broken glass out of the frame so he could see the entire photo, but he cut his finger. Exasperated, he smashed the frame against the bedpost. Glass tinkled to the floor, revealing the groom. Merrin gasped and felt a momentary dizziness. Hand-in-hand with Sarah, dressed in a tuxedo and looking serious, was—

A hand landed on Merrin's shoulder. He spun with a shout of surprise. Chuma stood behind him, a shotgun tucked under his arm.

"What's happening out there?" Merrin asked.

"The warriors are assembling in the hills," Chuma said. "The sandstorm will give them equal footing with the soldiers. The British have rifles, but they can't shoot what they can't see."

"Sarah went into the church when the dome first was uncovered, didn't she? *Didn't she*? With her husband." He turned the photo so Chuma could see it. "Anton Bession."

Merrin had been expecting disbelief or a floundering attempt at lying. Instead, Chuma looked mildly surprised. "No one told you they were married? Or perhaps you did not ask."

Realization struck Merrin like a bolt of lightning.

The picture and its frame crashed to the floor. "We've been deceived, Chuma. Joseph's not the one possessed. It's *Sarah*."

Chants rose and spun around the fire as Sebituana, his warriors, and the other tribal leaders whipped themselves into a war frenzy. Dozens upon dozens of visiting warriors danced and shouted, forming a seething mass of angry bodies. Knives flashed in the firelight as they cut and slashed at each other with the blades, giving each other a hundred tiny cuts and whooping in ecstacy as their blood splashed the flames. Their resentment toward the whites grew. It went beyond Jomo's death and the horror of Sebituana's son. The anger went back to the gold mine, the fighting, the loss of land and life.

"Remember the slavery," Sebituana cried.

"The slavery!" shouted the men.

"Remember the slaughter!"

"The slaughter!"

"Remember our revenge!"

"Revenge!"

Above them, the sky became a violent, murky green.

The wind intensified, carrying with it a stinging load of sand that burned the eyes of Father Will Francis, clogged his nose, and filled his mouth. Still, he was glad for it. The flying sand gave him extra cover as he circumnavigated the site to approach the church unnoticed by both Turkana warriors and British soldiers. Somehow he got the jeep close to the giant double doors without being noticed, prompting him to breathe a silent prayer of thanks. He shut the jeep off and gathered Joseph into his arms. The boy's skin was hot with fever, and the lesions had gotten worse. Will's heart was pounding hard enough to shake his shirt and make his Roman collar bob visibly, but he tried to move with confidence and faith. God was with him. God would see him through this. God would not abandon his servant.

The moment Will entered the church, the air went still, though it carried a stench of blood and bowel. The area around the altar was slick with both materials. Dead crows littered the floor. Will couldn't avoid treading on them. Their bodies crunched beneath his boots. He swallowed. He didn't know exactly what had happened to Jefferies, but it must have been hideous.

Joseph began to shake again. Another bestial moan emerged from his throat, and his teeth flashed white in the dim light. Will had a sudden image of Joseph snapping at his neck, tearing at the jugular. That urged him to hurry forward, passing the statues of the archangels huddled around the bloody altar . . . and failing to notice that the stone sword was missing from one of the Michaels.

Will paused at the bloody altar with the top stone askew. Unusable for his purposes. Flies bounced off his head and neck. He hadn't fully explored the upper structure, but he knew that most Byzantine churches put a baptismal font in one of the transepts—the short arms of the cross-shaped church. He checked in the north transept. Completely empty, except for a mosaic of a six-winged angel glaring at him from the wall. He checked the south transept, and there it was—a raised stone basin, easily large enough to contain a small child. Joseph's shaking intensified, and Will had a hard time holding him. He placed Joseph in the basin.

The boy vomited on him, sticky and green and steaming. Will leaped back with a cry. He yanked a handkerchief from his pocket, wiped off what he could, and tossed the handkerchief aside. Joseph went back to moaning in the basin, low, guttural sounds that echoed eerily around the church.

From his other pocket, Will drew a purple stole wrapped around a bottle of holy water. He kissed the stole once, then draped it around his neck. A black feather, caught on an errant draft, brushed his cheek and fluttered to the floor at his feet. Will tried to clear his mind of everything but prayer. It was difficult. Could he do this by himself? He had never performed an exorcism, didn't know anyone who had. He had read about them, of course, but the Vatican's current policy was to treat requests for exorcism with psychiatric help. Maybe he was wrong. Maybe Joseph was just sick. Maybe hyenas always ganged up on a single victim and ignored any others.

Then he thought about the crows in the church and events at the clinic. No. Satan's hand touched this place, these people, and the duty fell to Will to fight back.

But can *you?* whispered a doubting voice in his head. *You're nothing but a priest, not even ten years out of seminary. You're not a bishop or a cardinal. The ultimate evil* has permeated this site for millennia, *ever since Lucifer fell from grace and slammed into the earth with his wings on fire. What can you possibly do?*

"Begone, Satan," Will whispered, though his hands trembled. "You will not make me doubt."

I doubt that, laughed the treacherous little voice.

Will ignored it and opened *The Roman Book of Rituals.* "In the name of the Father, and of the Son, and of the Holy Spirit. Amen," he said, and began to read the prayer to Michael. "St. Michael the Archangel, illustrious leader of the heavenly army, defend us in the battle against principalities and powers, against the rulers of the world of darkness and the spirit of wickedness in high places. Come to the rescue of mankind, whom God has made in His own image and likeness, and purchased from Satan's tyranny at so great a price."

A shadow behind him shifted, revealing a face stretched wide by a glittering grin. Sarah slid from darkness, a stone sword in her hand. Her feet were bare, and they made no sound on the stone floor as she crept up behind Will. Her eyes were black as a moonless night.

"The Lord has entrusted to you the task of leading the souls of the redeemed to heavenly blessedness," Will prayed. "Entreat the Lord of peace to cast Satan down under our feet, so as to keep him from further holding man captive and doing harm to the Church. Carry our prayers up to God's throne, that the mercy of the Lord may quickly come and lay hold of the beast, the serpent of old, Satan and his demons, casting him in chains into the abyss, so that he can no longer seduce the nations."

He opened the bottle of holy water. Joseph moaned in the basin. Sarah slipped closer. Tensed and ready to fight, Will splashed some of the water on Joseph's face.

Nothing happened. Will frowned and splashed the boy again. The droplets merely washed a green bit of vomit from Joseph's chin. That wasn't right. The rites said that the afflicted couldn't bear the touch of blessed objects.

Cloth rustled behind him. Will whirled in time to see Sarah raise the stone sword. She brought it down. Will flung himself sideways, and the blade shattered on the marble floor. In a flash, Sarah was on top of him, her thighs pressing his upper body to the floor. Book and bottle went flying. Sarah's pretty face was twisted into an evil leer mere inches away from his own. Will struggled to fling her off, but she was surprisingly strong and heavy. Her knees pinned him down at the elbows, robbing him of leverage.

"It's you," he gasped. "Joseph was just touched, but you—"

"You should listen to your own advice, Father," she said in a low, throaty chuckle, then shifted her thighs. "Hmmmm . . . I like this. What happens, do you think, to a priest who breaks his vows while trying to invoke what measly power God grants him?"

She reached behind herself and ran a hand over his groin, her touch as light as a fly's. To his horror, Will found himself stiffening in response. He struggled to get up, without success. Sarah's touch grew more intense, and Will stifled a groan.

"No," he said with considerable effort. "Leave me . . . alone."

"But you don't want me to leave you alone, do you?" Sarah said huskily. She leaned down to whisper in his ear, and her breath was hot. "You're thinking that if I force you to impale me on your little spear, it won't really be breaking your vow of chastity. And you could find out what it's like to have a woman slide down on you without guilt. Isn't that right, Father?"

Will shook his head, though the gesture was an utter lie. He had never been with a woman in his entire life, had shunned it as wrong. Yet sometimes at night, when he lay on his stomach with the erect serpent throbbing beneath him, he wondered, fantasized, what it might be like. And sometimes he would rub himself back and forth on the mattress—not touching himself, as was forbidden and wrong. Just rubbing. Rubbing back and forth until he burst, all the time thinking of what it was like to do it with someone beneath him. And afterward, regular as the sunrise, came guilt, confession, and penance.

"Would there be guilt and penance this time, Father?" Sarah cooed. Her hand traced the outline of his erection through his trousers. Will had never felt anyone's hands on him before, and the sensation brought a strange coppery taste to his mouth. Shivers ran up and down his body. He inhaled sharply as Sarah gripped him with a firm hand and wagged playfully. It would be so easy to give in. What could be wrong with it if he was forced?

"You'll *love* it, Father," she whispered, "and you'll be guilt-free."

Then he caught sight of the giant crucifix, still hanging upside down from its chain. The devil twisted words, turned them upside down as it had the crucifix. How could he believe anything Satan said?

"No!" he shouted, and flung himself upward. The move caught Sarah by surprise, and she flew backward off him. She twisted like a tiger in midair and was on her feet before he was. Before Will could recover his balance, she backhanded him across the face. The blow smashed him flat again. Dazed, Will scrambled to recover his wits. He reached for the bottle of holy water, but Sarah's foot crashed down on his hand, snapping his fingers. As he howled in agony, Sarah kicked him in the face. His head snapped back, and he landed on the cold floor again. Joseph was still moaning in the baptismal font.

"Shut up!" Sarah snarled, and the boy fell silent again.

Hot pain thundered through Will's head, and he couldn't seem to think straight. He tried to sit up, but his body wouldn't obey. The church floor rocked and swayed beneath him. Something moved above him and he looked up. Sarah stood over him with a stone spear, another Michael weapon.

"How many angels can dance on the head of a pin, Father?" Sarah aimed the point at Will's chest a little to the left of the midline and brought the spear down. Will caught the shaft in both hands and tried to push back, but Sarah was strong, so strong. The tip came inexorably down toward his chest, piercing his shirt and pricking the skin just above his heart. Will's arms trembled with the effort of holding her back.

"Begone . . . Satan," gasped Father William Francis.

"We've heard that before," Sarah rasped. "That's why we're down here instead of up there." And she rammed the spear home.

Twelve

✝

The village of Derati, British East Africa

The possessor may become dispossessed.
—Kenyan proverb

THE SANDSTORM CREATED a twilight that nipped and scratched at anyone who ventured outside. At the edge of the dig site, a line of British troops waited, handkerchiefs tied over their lower faces in an attempt to filter out the dust and sand. They were using rocks and boulders for rough cover, though it was still hard to see—and be seen—through the blowing sand.

A shadow moved within the clouds of dust. Before any of the soldiers could raise an alarm, a mob of Turkana warriors burst from the darkness, their howls mingling with the storm's. The soldiers immediately opened fire, but the Turkana were almost on top of them. Half a dozen warriors fell, but the rest rushed ahead, flinging heavy spears and drawing sharp machetes. One spear sheared off the top of a soldier's head. A Turkana jerked to a halt and stared down at the blood gushing from his chest before collapsing to the ground. Another Turkana swung his machete with angry force and decapitated a redheaded soldier, only to fall to a bayonet shoved into his back. The carnage continued, with both sides snarling like rabid animals in a frenzy. The wind screamed and laughed like a living thing and covered up blood, bone, and brain with a fine layer of desert sand.

Merrin fled out the hospital door with the heavy idol in his hands. Chuma, still armed with the shotgun, came close on his heels. The sandstorm struck like a living thing, tearing at face and skin. The two men ran for the lorry parked a little ways up the street. Whirling sand made it hard to see. Merrin had just reached the driver's door when out of the blinding sand burst a Turkana warrior, heavy spear raised. He was right behind Chuma.

"No!" Merrin shouted. "Chuma!"

The foreman spun and raised his shotgun at the same moment the warrior slammed his spear straight through Chuma's chest. The head emerged from Chuma's back with a terrible, wet sound. Chuma gave a small gasp, then jerked the shotgun's trigger. The blast ripped the warrior in half, spraying the lorry with blood. Both men went down. Chuma twitched once and lay still.

Merrin clutched the idol to his chest and stared at the two mangled bodies lying at his feet. He felt a rising panic, then a strange calm. Chuma was dead, but Joseph was still alive. He could still save Joseph.

Merrin snatched up Chuma's shotgun, flung it into the lorry's cab along with the idol, and followed them inside. With shaking hands he cranked the engine to life and stamped on the accelerator. He hit the headlights, but the twin beams barely cut through the dim light, creating a narrow tunnel for him to drive through as he left the village. Wind and sand tore at the vehicle, and gritty air washed over Merrin's sweaty face and back. The bumpy, uneven back route forced him to drive slower, and he railed at the delay. Sarah was possessed. The devil was real. And if the devil was real, that meant—

The sandstorm parted, and a pack of hyenas appeared on the road. Merrin slammed on the brakes, sending the lorry into a skid. It slid several feet, then stopped. The shotgun and the idol tumbled to the floorboards. There were six of the beasts, jaws open, green eyes glittering in the headlights. They stared straight at him. Merrin swallowed dryly and his palms began to sweat. He could gun the motor and drive straight over them, but these were large animals. Their bodies might cripple the lorry. The hyenas panted, and their tongues lolled mockingly in the moaning wind. Then one of them began to laugh. The others joined in. It was a cold, merciless sound that puckered Merrin's skin. If he hit the accelerator, would they move out of the way? He bit his lip and thought, *Only one way to—*

A crash of broken glass. Shards and shrapnel showered Merrin's face and he gave a yelp of fear. A hyena landed on the seat next to him. It had leaped through the passenger window. Its lips pulled back from long teeth that dripped saliva, and Merrin smelled its breath, foul and fetid with rotten meat. The shotgun was out of reach, and fear froze Merrin at the wheel.

The predator's massive body took up most of the cabin. It leaned closer, and its breath was cold. Merrin desperately cast about for a weapon, but saw nothing. The hyena laughed bright and hard, right in Merrin's ear. Cool saliva sprayed over him, and the animal leaned closer, as if to give Merrin a kiss. It opened its mouth wider, ready to sink its fangs into his neck. And then Merrin's hand came out of his pocket holding Francis's vial of holy water.

"Get thee behind me!" he shouted, and emptied the contents into the hyena's face.

The hyena screamed. Flesh hissed, and thin tendrils of smoke rose from its muzzle. It screamed again, then turned and fled out the broken window, leaving a streak of bone-white feces on the seat. Merrin slammed the accelerator to the floor. The lorry leaped forward, forcing the remaining hyena pack to scatter. A moment later, Merrin risked a glance into his rearview mirror. Five pairs of green eyes glowered malevolently in the semidarkness.

He arrived at the dig site with the storm whirling and rushing around him like an afreet gone mad. Sand scratched his skin beneath his clothes. His mouth and ears were full of grit. Merrin grabbed the idol and leaped down from the lorry. The church loomed ahead of him, a low, dark shade in the swirling sand. Merrin lurched forward against the storm. Bodies, dozens of them, were piled everywhere. Turkana spears pointed upward from corpses like broken fingers. Ropes of bowel looped around bodies slashed open by machetes and bayonets. Empty eyes stared out of severed heads. Merrin accidentally kicked one, and it rolled away like a misshapen football. Further away, from a place swallowed by the storm, Merrin heard gunshots and screams. The battle had not yet ended.

A hyena appeared out of the howling sand, dragging a soldier by the leg. The man was shrieking in fear and pain. Merrin dropped the idol and raised the shotgun. Even if he missed, the shot might frighten the animal off. He pulled the trigger, but the gun only made a muffled click. It was clogged with sand and wouldn't fire. The hyena vanished into the storm, hauling the hapless soldier with it. Merrin threw the shotgun aside and bent down to retrieve the idol. It was already nearly buried. He started to dig for it. Five more hyenas emerged from the wall of wind, chuckling among themselves as they slunk closer. Heart pounding, Merrin abandoned the idol and ran into the church.

The storm cut off so abruptly, Merrin stumbled. He stood in the entryway, brushing sand from his hair and shaking it from his clothes. He wanted a long, hot bath and a tall, cold drink. He wanted to be back in England, where the weather was cool and wet. He wanted Chuma alive again.

Wishes and horses, he told himself. *Keep moving.*

He pulled the big doors shut behind him, then moved up the aisle toward the archangel statues, slowly, so his eyes could adjust to the dim light let in by the dome. The statues looked strange. He smelled blood, and he thought he'd never get that scent out of his nose again. Feathers rustled in the shadows. As Merrin drew closer to the nave, he saw what was wrong. The statues and the floor around them were covered with crows, hundreds and hundreds of crows. They hunched in eerie silence, and every one of them was staring at Merrin. His mouth felt dry, and he had to force himself to press forward.

The giant crucifix had moved. It was still upside down, but now it hung directly above the altar. It, too, was covered with silent crows.

"Francis?" Merrin called. "Joseph?" He paused. "Sarah?"

He edged around the circle of angels. The altar lay open, the stone staircase leading downward. Merrin spotted a lantern—Francis's?—glowing on the floor. He snatched it up and shone it around the transepts. The crows turned their heads to follow him, but didn't otherwise move. The light picked out the baptismal font. It was slicked with blood, but whose? He stepped closer. On the ground lay a crucifix on a neck chain. Francis's. Beside it was *The Book of Roman Rituals* and the bottle of holy water. It had tipped on its side, and some of the contents had dribbled onto the floor. Merrin dipped his finger in the puddle. With a shaky hand he made the sign of the cross on his forehead. He rescued the bottle, the remaining holy water sloshing around as he capped and pocketed it.

For the first time in five years, Lankester Merrin knelt to pray. The floor was hard on his knees. He clasped his hands and bowed his head. What should he say? How did you speak to someone you've turned your back on? Words refused to come at first. And then verses from the Book of Matthew leaped into his mind.

"Lord, forgive me my disbelief," he whispered. "Take my disbelief into Your bosom, O Lord, and give me strength." The words weren't exact, but it was the sentiment that counted. "Hear my prayer. I need You. These people need You. This valley needs You. You must hear my cry. Do not abandon us now. Absolve my sins and purify me for this task. Lord, forgive my disbelief."

He repeated the prayer in different forms three times. During the final recitation, he felt like he was clawing his way through earth, fighting to get to the surface before he suffocated.

"Lord," Merrin said for the third and final time, "forgive my disbelief!"

He waited. Nothing. Well, he couldn't expect the heavens to open and the trumpets to sound. Merrin got to his feet, grimacing at the pain in his knees. He kissed Francis's cross and slipped it around his neck. Clutching *The Book of Roman Rituals*, he turned and froze.

The crows were gone. Not even a feather marked their presence. Merrin's heart did a little leap. Was it a sign? Or just a coincidence? He decided to take it as a sign, and he added a mental thanks to God.

Then he saw the blood trail. Someone had dragged a large, bloody object—a body—over the floor toward the statues. Beside the trail was a set of smaller footprints. Child-sized. Joseph-sized. Merrin's own blood ran cold.

He followed the trail back to the angels. A choked, whimpering cry reached his ears. Merrin peered around one of the Michaels. Joseph was sitting on the edge of the altar above the staircase, eyes wide with terror.

Merrin stepped toward him. "Joseph—"

Scarlet dripped over the boy in a steady rain. Slowly, heart pounding, Merrin shone his lantern upward. Blood was flowing across the face of Jesus from no source Merrin could see. He raised the light higher.

Sarah lounged on the crossbar as if it were a comfortable sofa. Her skin was mottled and gray, and her mouth stretched wide as a frog's. Beneath her, Jesus continued to bleed.

"Come sit with us, Lankester," she cooed. "I promise we won't bite."

Merrin staggered, then forced himself upright. God was with him. "Joseph," he whispered. "Run!"

The boy tensed to obey, but Sarah swung down to face him, hanging upside down like a bat. She waggled an admonishing finger at Joseph, who froze again.

"Leave him alone," Merrin said.

Bones creaked as Sarah—no, the *demon*—twisted around at an impossible angle to look at him. Her—its—eyes were black pools and showed no white at all. "Make me."

Merrin set down the lantern and opened the book of rituals. " 'Lord, have mercy,' " he read. " 'Christ, have mercy. Lord, have mercy. Christ, hear us. God, the Father in Heaven, have mercy on us. God, the Son, Redeemer of the world, have mercy on us.' "

"It's not working," the demon growled.

" 'God the Holy Ghost, have mercy on us. Holy Trinity, One God, have mercy on us. Holy Mary, pray for us.' "

A rush of air, and the demon dropped down from the cross. It stepped toward Merrin, its movements predatory and sensual. Merrin took a step back, then caught himself and stayed his ground.

The demon licked its lips with a gray tongue. "What's the matter, Merrin? Don't you want to fuck me anymore?"

It reached out to touch Merrin's face. His hand snapped out and caught the demon by the wrist. The creature laughed like a hyena, and its breath was carrion cold and nauseating. The movement displayed the numbers tattooed on Sarah's forearm. Before Merrin's eyes, they squirmed and shifted like worms, transforming into *Ratują mnie*. Merrin knew enough Polish to translate.

Save me.

Merrin's jaw firmed. He would obey. " 'All ye Holy Patriarchs and Prophets, pray for us. St. Peter, pray for us. St. Paul, pray for us. St. Andrew, pray for us.' "

"You are a weak vessel, Merrin," the demon purred. "What makes you think God would grant *you* the power to cleanse this place? You let all those people die. You turned your back on God. Why would he listen to you? You, who believe in nothing? You're alone here, Merrin. Without love, without friends, without hope."

The words struck Merrin like stone daggers. He *was* a weak vessel. He had failed in Hellendoorn, failed, and that fact filled him with a black ocean of shame and guilt. He had no hope against a demon this powerful, against a demon of any kind. Why would God want to work through something so weak and impure? He started to close *The Book of Roman Rituals*. Then his eye fell on Joseph, wide-eyed and bloody on the altar, like a lamb awaiting sacrifice. A true innocent. Iron resolve hardened inside Merrin. He might have failed Hellendoorn, but he would not fail Sarah or this boy.

"If God has refused to work through me, demon," Merrin snarled, "why are you afraid of me?" In a swift movement, he grabbed the demon's head with both hands and pressed their foreheads together. Francis's book fell to the floor. The demon screamed as the holy water cross he had painted there seared its skin.

"Almighty Lord, the Father of Jesus Christ, God and Lord of all creation," Merrin boomed into the creature's face, "grant me, Your unworthy servant, pardon for all my sins, and the power to confront this cruel demon."

The demon vomited, spraying Merrin's face with cold green sputum. Its fingernails raked Merrin's cheeks, but he didn't let go.

"I command you by the judge of the living and the dead," he shouted, "to depart from this servant of God. It is the power of Christ that compels you!"

And then Merrin was holding Lieutenant Kessel's head against his own. The Nazi officer grinned a grin full of black, rotting teeth.

"God is not here today, priest," he gurgled.

Merrin couldn't stop himself from flinching. In that

moment, the demon broke free and shoved him hard. Merrin crashed to the ground, slid, and cracked his head against one of the statues. Stars of pain burst across his retina. By the time his head cleared and he managed to sit up, the demon was gone. Head pounding in time with his heart, he snatched up the lantern and shone it around the church. No sign of the creature. Joseph, to his relief, still sat on the open altar. Merrin held out his hand.

"Joseph," he said. "Come to me."

The boy shook his head, tears streaming down his face and mingling with the blood from the crucifix. Merrin moved toward him as if he were a skittish animal.

"Joseph, you must come now," he said in a soothing voice. "It's time to leave. Do you want to leave?"

A pause. Then the boy nodded, his eyes darting about in fear. But as he started to slide off the stone, a gray hand shot out of the altar behind him. It yanked the boy backward into the stairwell. He didn't even scream.

"No!" Merrin dove for the altar, but Joseph was already gone. Demonic laughter echoed from the stairs, growing fainter in the distance. Merrin didn't hesitate. He stuffed *The Book of Roman Rituals* into his pocket and clattered down the stairs as fast as he could. In the foyer at the bottom, the round rock had been rolled aside. Merrin entered the temple. His lantern was the only source of illumination, and the stygian darkness seemed to swallow even that light.

"Yea, though I walk through the valley of the shadow

217

of death," he said in a firm voice, "I will fear no evil, for Thou art with me, my Lord."

Running footsteps pelted by in the blackness. Merrin swung the lantern, trying to catch the person who made them. There was a grinding sound, then silence. Merrin's sweeping light revealed nothing but the demonic carvings and ancient altar. New blood ran in rivulets across its grooved surface and dripped into the pit next to it. Merrin wondered what would happen if he chanted the spiral spell he was standing on, but decided against finding out. He had to find Joseph before the demon—

Something gleamed on the floor. It was the rock hammer Merrin had given Joseph. It lay directly beneath the statue of the lion-headed, winged man. The archaeologist part of Merrin's mind finally produced a name for it—Pazuzu, Sumerian god of disease and ill winds.

Merrin picked up the hammer, then looked at the statue. The idol was supposed to sit in the recess carved into the statue's abdomen, and it was meant to face inward. Earlier, the arrangement had struck Merrin as a key-and-lock sort of fit. He felt around the inside of the recess, then poked his fingers into the sockets where the idol's eyes would go. He pushed with all his strength.

The statue shifted, just slightly. Merrin shifted his grip and pushed sideways. The statue moved with the low grinding sound Merrin had heard earlier. He pointed the lantern at the wall behind the statue and found a crevice in the rock barely wide enough to grant passage. Merrin breathed deeply, then stepped inside.

Stone closed in around him like a coffin. The only sound was his breathing, harsh and heavy in his own ears.

"Joseph?" he tried to call. It came out as a hoarse whisper. His heart thundered inside his ears, and every nerve he had screamed at him to hurry, to run, find the demon before it killed Joseph—or worse.

"O God, by Your name, save me," Merrin said. "By Your strength, defend my cause."

He moved down the narrow tunnel. Ten yards. Twenty. He heard breathing behind him, almost in his ear. He whipped the lantern around, nearly cracking it against the tunnel wall. A brief glimpse of the demon's face flicked into view, then vanished. Merrin stood there for a moment, too afraid to move forward, too frightened to go back.

"Turn back the evil upon my foes," he said. "In Your faithfulness destroy them. Because from all distress you have rescued me, and my eyes look down upon my enemies."

Steeling himself, Merrin moved ahead, carefully at first, then gaining speed. His feet told him he was walking on something . . . familiar. Merrin slowed and swept the lantern downward to check. Bumpy cobblestones made the tunnel floor. A dusting of snow glittered on them. His chest tightened. Ahead of him, he heard singing. It was a girl's voice, sweet and light. Merrin recognized her—Aartje Kroon, the girl shot by Kessel. She had red-blond hair in braids and wore a simple blue dress. And she was standing at what appeared to be the mouth of the tunnel Merrin was in.

Merrin started to run, lantern bobbing. A part of him screamed that it was a trick, but he couldn't help himself. If he could catch her, he might be able to save her this time.

"Aartje!" he called out.

The girl smiled at Merrin and waved. He was almost to her, could almost touch her. Abruptly he was slammed to the ground beneath an enormous, lumpy object. A wet human body pressed him to the floor, heavy and suffocating. Merrin smelled sand and felt sticky cloth against his face. He fought and clawed at it to free himself. When he was able to shove the corpse aside, he shone the light on it. It was the dead Nazi from Hellendoorn, clad in black with a silver insignia on his collar. Merrin dropped the lantern and the light dimmed to a spark. Blackness closed in. Merrin felt around desperately, his hands unable to avoid touching the corpse. Its skin was cold and wet. He felt dead fingers beneath his own. At last—at *last*—he found the lantern and shook it back to life.

The corpse was of William Francis. A great hole gaped in his chest, and Merrin remembered the bleeding Jesus. Francis's jaw hung slack. Merrin scrambled backward, swallowing to keep the nausea down.

"Father . . ." he muttered, feeling devastated and empty. For all that he had infuriated Merrin, Will Francis was—had been—a good man, and a good priest. Certainly better than Merrin had been. Anger rose inside Merrin.

"God and Father of our Lord Jesus Christ," he said, "I appeal to Your Holy name, humbly begging Your kind-

220

ness, that You graciously grant me help against this and every unclean spirit now tormenting this creature of Yours; through Christ our Lord."

He leaned down and murmured a soft prayer over the body, last rites for a dead man's soul. Then he carefully, respectfully removed the purple stole from its place around Francis's neck. It was free of blood, and Merrin decided to take that as another sign. He kissed it with reverence and placed it around his own neck.

A few more feet down the tunnel, Merrin emerged into an open space. The ceiling was so high, the lantern light couldn't reach it. The floor was normal cave stone. Three tunnels faced him, all three leading into pitch blackness. There was no sign of the demon or of Joseph. Merrin played the light over each tunnel entrance, trying to decide what to do.

"Father!" It was Joseph's voice. Merrin's heart leaped. He tried to locate the source, but the word bounced and echoed all around. "Father!" The word was fainter this time.

"Joseph!" Merrin ran forward. "Joseph, I'm coming!"

Which one? Which one? In desperation Merrin shone the lantern at the base of each tunnel, hoping against hope there might be something that would leave a footprint, some kind of clue.

A flicker of movement shifted within the middle tunnel. Merrin plunged into it. The roof sloped down sharply, almost immediately forcing Merrin to crawl. "Joseph!" he cried again.

"Father, please!" came Joseph's voice, far ahead of him. "She has me. I'm scared!"

Merrin's breathing grew harsh in his ears as he crawled forward. The tunnel ceiling came down lower, forcing him to snake ahead on his stomach. He could feel the hard, unyielding stone around him—no place to stand up, no place to turn around. Claustrophobia stole over him, but he kept moving forward. A moaning growl came behind him. Merrin jumped, banging his head on the ceiling. He tried to twist around, but the tunnel was too narrow. His feet and legs felt vulnerable, and he remembered the hyena dragging the soldier away.

"O God, hear my prayer," Merrin said. "Listen to the words of my mouth. The arrogant have risen against me; the ruthless seek my life; they do not keep God before them."

The moaning growl came again, right on Merrin's heels. He kicked backward as best he could, but hit nothing. Merrin wanted to scream, let himself go insane from the stress and fear, but he wormed his way forward another yard.

"God and Father of our Lord Jesus Christ," he panted, "I appeal to Your Holy name, humbly begging Your kindness, that You graciously grant me help against this and every unclean spirit now tormenting this creature of Yours; through Christ our Lord."

The lantern dimmed. Merrin felt panic rise. Trapped beneath the earth, locked beneath tons of rock in total darkness with a demon. Trying to keep calm, he blew softly on the dimming flame, trying to coax it back to brightness.

It went out. Merrin lay alone in utter blackness with

unyielding stone walls hard in around him. His breathing came hard and fast and he felt dizzy. He tapped the lantern, hoping against hope that it would—

The lantern burst into full illumination and Merrin looked straight into the demon's nightmare face. He tried to rear back, but there was nowhere to go. The demon's nails slashed his face. The pain seared his skin and he felt warmth trickle down his cheek. He tried to raise his hands in a defensive gesture, fight her off, but he had no room to move. The demon howled with glee and slashed again and again. Desperately Merrin struggled to pull the bottle of holy water from his pocket, but he couldn't quite reach it. "O Holy Lord, Almighty Father, eternal God and Father of our Lord Jesus Christ," he shouted, "who didst one time consign that fugitive and fallen tyrant to everlasting hellfire—"

And then the bottle was in his hand. He flicked it open and splashed it into the demon's eyes. Flesh hissed and bubbled. Its eyes bleeding black tears, the creature shrieked and recoiled, sucking itself backward like a frightened worm.

"—strike terror, O Lord, into the beast that lays waste Thy vineyard." Merrin tried to splash again, but the demon's hand snapped forward and caught his wrist. It yanked Merrin forward, and only then did he realize that only the upper part of the demon's body had been inside the tunnel. For a terrifying second he dropped in freefall, then slammed hard onto a rocky floor. The holy water bottle skittered away, but by some miracle he kept hold of the lantern. Before Merrin could recover, strong arms grabbed him from behind and spun him sideways. He smashed into a cave wall and slid to the ground. The lantern landed upright beside him, offering barely enough light to see by.

"How can you call on Him when you're so much closer to *me*?" the demon growled.

Battered and bleeding, Merrin struggled to rise, but the demon slammed him back down again with little effort. It landed hard on his chest, brought its face inches from his. Black ichor dripped on Merrin's bloody face.

"From all evil . . . O Lord, . . . deliver us," he gasped. "From Thy wrath . . . deliver us. From all sin, deliver us." The words were giving him strength. "From sudden and unprovided death, deliver us. From the snares of the devil—"

"Snares, Father?" the demon said. "I set no snares. You come to me of your own free will. Death times ten."

"—deliver us. From anger, hatred, and all ill will, deliver us. From all lewdness, deliver us."

"Lewdness like you felt with Sarah?" the demon leered. "Tell me, Merrin—would God accept the return of a priest who only days before had a raging hard-on for a woman? The original sin, Father."

"From lightning and tempest, deliver us. From the scourge of earthquakes, deliver us."

The demon leaned down and whispered in Merrin's ear, "Don't you want to go back?"

"From plague, famine, and war, deliver us." *Go back?*

"Yesss," the demon hissed. "Go back. You can undo the events of that day, Father. You can end your guilt."

No. "From everlasting death, deliver us."

"You want to," the demon said, and it wasn't asking a question. "You do."

"By the mystery . . . by . . . by . . ." The words faltered. Suddenly Merrin had a vision of himself standing next to Kessel, of wrestling the gun away from him, saying something witty even as he shot the man in the face. It was wrong. Vengeance was for God, not for man. But the idea wouldn't leave him alone. It hung before him, easy and tempting. He . . . he . . . *wanted* . . .

There was a wrench, and now Merrin was standing in gray drizzle. The cobblestones were hard beneath his feet, and the air was chill and damp. No demon. Only villagers in a damp huddle, surrounded by armed soldiers. An open-eyed corpse in a Nazi uniform lay on the street. Lieutenant Kessel, his hawk face and black uniform wet with rain, twisted his face into what was supposed to be a smile.

"You. Priest," he snapped. "What is your name?"

The words rolled off his tongue. "I am Father Merrin."

"These . . . creatures are your parish?"

Merrin's head dipped in a nod. This wasn't right. He wasn't supposed to be here. But where else would he be?

"They confess to you, then," Kessel continued. "So. Point out the one responsible."

"No one here did this, Lieutenant. They aren't capable of it."

"Didn't you hear what I said?"

"That God is not here today," Merrin replied steadily. "Yes, I know that."

Kessel paused as if confused, as if that hadn't been the expected response. In a flash Merrin knew what was coming. Or was he remembering it?

Kessel turned to the frightened villagers. "I am going to shoot ten of you," he boomed, "in the hope that we can demonstrate to this wretch the terrible responsibility he has incurred." Kessel scanned the crowd and settled on a man in his thirties. Merrin recognized Nico Tuur. The SS officer drew his pistol, yanked Nico from the crowd, and forced him to his knees on the street. The other soldiers aimed their weapons at the remaining villagers.

"You have big hands," Kessel said, putting the barrel of his pistol to Nico's temple. Nico swallowed visibly. "A farmer. Do you have children?"

"Yes," Nico whispered. "Two girls."

"Excellent. We'll start with you."

"Stop!" Merrin shouted.

Kessel turned without moving his gun. "You have some objection, priest?"

"I killed your man," Merrin declared. "Shoot me."

"Yes," Kessel said with a reptilian smile. "You'd like that. The good shepherd offers to die so that his sheep may live. But I think not. I want you to choose, priest. You have five seconds."

"I . . . can't," Merrin whispered. It was happening all over again. He had run this scene through his mind thousands and thousands of times, things he could have said, things he could have done. Why were none of them coming to him now?

Kessel reached out and grabbed the nearest person to

him, a teenaged girl named Aartje Kroon. He brought the pistol up—

—and Merrin lunged. Before any of the startled Nazis could react, he grabbed Kessel's hand and twisted hard. The lieutenant yelled in pain, and suddenly Merrin was holding the gun. With a triumphant smile, he aimed it at the lieutenant. The villagers milled about uncertainly.

"Tell your men to lay down their weapons and leave!" Merrin barked. "If you don't, priest or no, I swear I'll kill you!"

Kessel's eyes went to the barrel of the pistol, then to Merrin's face. "Get what satisfaction you can, priest, because my men will not lay down their weapons."

The German soldiers raised their rifles and trained them on the villagers. Without another thought, Merrin pulled the trigger. Blood and brain exploded from Kessel's head. He dropped like a dead doll and landed in a puddle with a splash.

"Fire!" a German voice called out. "Fire! Kill them all!"

"No!" Merrin cried. He turned just in time to see the rifles spit and bark. Aartje Kroon was the first to fall, her face a mask of shock and pain. Nico Tuur was next. A German soldier aimed his rifle straight at Merrin. Before he could react, the man fired. The impact flung Merrin backward. He landed hard but, oddly, felt no pain. He was able to see the Nazis continue to shoot, cutting the villagers down like winter wheat until not one was left. Merrin's eyes grew heavy, and they closed.

He was lying on a hard stone surface, and his clothes

were dry. He lay there for a long time, waiting to die, but nothing happened. Slowly, Merrin opened his eyes and sat up. He was back in the cave. He put a hand to his chest and felt the deep wound. Then it moved beneath his hand and he felt the edges melt seamlessly together. Merrin pulled his hand away. The blood on his palm vanished. The lantern sat on the floor beside him, still shedding a glow. If he ever got back, he would have to enshrine it.

"Feel better?" the demon purred. It crouched like a gargoyle on the floor in front of Merrin. "You did what you could. You laid down your life, but God decided to kill them anyway. Not just the ten you chose the first time, but all of them. You see? Your guilt is gone. You are free."

"Free not to care?" he asked.

"Free to walk this earth your own man, without debt or guilt."

Merrin hesitated. It was true. No matter what he might have done, the villagers had been doomed to die. No matter what he did down here, a war was going to begin up there. He didn't need to be involved. He didn't need to care. It would be so easy.

"That's right," the demon soothed. "Feel the peace. Feel the tranquillity. God doesn't care one way or the other. He has His own plan."

"And what if that plan includes me?" Merrin said suddenly.

"It doesn't," the demon countered. "Why would God make you suffer so much? Why put you through so much pain? Either God doesn't care, or He's simply cruel."

"Or He wanted me to be in this place at this time," Merrin said, voice rising. "To cleanse this place. To fight you in His name. This earth is not your dominion, evil one. Man is the chosen temple of God!"

A feeling of exultation swept through Merrin. He leaped to his feet and pointed at the demon. "In the name and by the power of our Lord Jesus Christ, let you be snatched away and driven from the Church of God!"

The demon howled and attacked. It crashed into Merrin and drove him to the floor, raking at him with its nails again. Merrin struggled beneath the weight, unable to dislodge it. The creature grabbed his head and slammed it against the stones. Pain burst through Merrin's skull and he saw stars.

The demon pressed its face forward, breathing into Merrin's open mouth as it spoke. "Where's your God now, Merrin? I'll tell you. He's fucking His only Son on His heavenly throne while you call out His name."

Merrin got an arm up and rammed the heel of his hand into the demon's forehead. It jerked backward, and he scrambled free. He backed several steps away.

"From the souls made to the image and likeness of God and redeemed by the Precious Blood of the Divine Lamb," Merrin shouted, "I cast you *out!*"

The demon gathered itself to attack—

—then halted and looked confused. It actually backed up a step.

"You're a killer, Merrin," it said, but its voice was hoarse. "You looked them in the eye and pointed your finger and they died. Because of you. God is not here today, priest."

Merrin whipped off his stole and jumped forward to press it to the creature's forehead. It screamed and leaped backward in an impossible arc, landing next to a large boulder.

"In the name of the Archangel Michael, in the name of Christ and His Saints, I cast thee out!"

The demon pressed itself against the rear wall of the cave, trembling and shaking. Savage growls issued from its throat.

"In the name of the Lord Jesus Christ! It is He who commands you! He who flung you from the heights of heaven to the depths of hell! Begone from this creature of—"

The demon's hand flashed down behind the boulder and yanked Joseph out of hiding. Its fingers wrapped tight around his throat and its nails pierced his flesh. Joseph made a whimpering choke, begging Merrin with his eyes.

"No," Merrin said, taking a step forward. The demon negligently twisted Joseph's head sideways. Merrin heard the vertebrae creak and froze.

"You're going to watch him die, Merrin," the demon said. "You're going to fail him like you failed all the others."

"No," Merrin said firmly. "I won't." He raised his voice and stepped forward again. "God, spare this child. For he is innocent and deserves Your blessing." The demon's fingers tensed, increasing the pressure, but Merrin didn't retreat.

"Spare this child," he repeated, "for he is innocent and deserves Your blessing!"

The creature's grip faltered. For a tiny moment, Sarah's normal face replaced the demon's visage. In that moment, Merrin ripped Joseph away and flung him to safety. Then he wrapped his arms around Sarah as the demon slammed back into existence with insane fury. It howled and scratched at Merrin's back like a crazed lover.

"I command you in the name of Christ to depart from this servant of God!" he bellowed. "It is the power of Christ that compels you!"

The demon went berserk, bucking and roaring with a thousand voices. Merrin held on with all his might.

"Why, Joseph?" came a voice from the blackness.

Merrin threw a glance over his shoulder. James stood in the dim light, his face and body torn and disfigured. His chest hung open, revealing white ribs and a beating heart. The ruin reached out to his little brother, who was standing by the lantern. Joseph shrank away with a cry.

"Why didn't you help me?" James asked in a bubbly wreck of a voice.

"Don't look, Joseph!" Merrin shouted. "It feeds off despair!"

Joseph spun around and buried his face in his hands. The demon bucked and howled in Merrin's grip, but he kept his arms wrapped around it like stones.

"It's God himself who commands you!" he yelled. "The majestic Christ who commands you! God the Father commands you! God the Son commands you!"

The demon went into convulsions. It threw up again, but this time it was only a faint, pasty film. Its groans were weakening. James tried to speak to his brother, but no sound came out of his mouth.

"God the Holy Spirit commands you! The mystery of the Cross commands you! The blood of the martyrs commands you! *Unclean spirit, I cast you out!*"

James vanished and the demon collapsed in Merrin's arms. He was holding Sarah Novack instead. Sobs wracked her body. A rush of fatigue swept over Merrin, and he lowered himself and Sarah to the cave floor. She wept hard, tears dripping on stone with a tiny tapping sound. Joseph scrambled over to join them. Merrin put one arm around him and held Sarah tight with the other. He felt tears gather in his own eyes as he stroked Sarah's hair.

"It's all right," he told them, and turned to Joseph. "You're all right. It's over."

Fear crossed Joseph's face. Merrin looked at him, puzzled. Then he became aware that his other hand was slick. He was stroking Aartje Kroon's bloody hair, her ruined head cradled on his shoulder.

Before he could react, the figure snapped back into the gray-faced demon in Sarah's body. The creature exploded from Merrin's arms, sending him flying backward across the cave. He landed hard, and the air whuffed out of him. He scrambled to his feet, adrenaline surging through him. Joseph ran to hide behind him. A thousand roars mingled with a million whispers erupted around them, swirling and confusing as desert sand. The demon was nowhere to be seen, but Merrin could feel its malevolent presence.

"Joseph," he said shakily, "I need you to help me. To

read with me. Whatever you hear, whatever you see—
it's just his lies. You must focus. We must be strong. Do
you understand?"

Joseph looked up at Merrin and their eyes met.
Merrin saw a hardness there, a hardness no little boy
should have, and his anger grew strong.

"I understand," Joseph said.

Merrin picked up *The Book of Roman Rituals* from
the spot where it had fallen to the floor. The demon's
roar intensified, and Merrin's head began to ache.
Holding the book open so the lantern light fell on the
page, he began to read.

" 'O God, by Your name, save me. By Your strength,
defend my cause. As it was in the beginning, is now and
ever shall be, world without end . . .' "

" 'Amen,' " Joseph read.

" 'Save Your servant . . .' "

" 'Who places his trust in Thee, my God.' "
Joseph's voice was high-pitched but firm. A cold
breeze stirred the air, stealing down Merrin's back
like an icy hand.

" 'Be unto Sarah, O Lord, a fortified tower . . .' "
Merrin read.

" 'In the face of the enemy.' "

" 'Let the enemy have no power over her. See the
Cross of the Lord." Merrin's voice rose to be heard over
the echoing roar. Wind whipped his hair and threat-
ened to blast the book out of his hands, but he could
feel the power rising within him like liquid light.
" 'Begone, you hostile power! O Lord, hear my
prayer!' "

" 'And let my cry come unto Thee!' " Joseph shouted.

" 'In the name of Archangel Michael, in the name of Christ and His saints, I cast thee out!' " Power and conviction swelled within Merrin and spilled over to flood the cave. His headache disappeared, his wounds stopped hurting. He stood here, in this place, as a servant to the Lord, and nothing could stop him.

" 'In the name of the Lord Jesus Christ! It is He who commands you! He who flung you from the heights of heaven to the depths of hell! Begone from this creature of God—' "

"Father!" Joseph shrieked.

From the far distant side of the cave charged a vision from hell. Merrin barely recognized Sarah's body. The creature barreled toward him on twisted legs. Long, greasy hair streamed behind it. Its eyes blazed like green acid, its mouth hung open. A forked, gray tongue protruded from between pointed teeth. Sharp, filthy claws reached out like hungry knives. A banshee wail screamed over Merrin, freezing his marrow. Every nerve howled at him to run, to flee for safety. Instead he forced himself to step forward and push Joseph behind him. The creature surged toward him, claws ready to slice him to pieces like a desert sandstorm.

"Begone!" he bellowed. "In the name of the Father, and of the Son, and of the Holy Spirit!"

The demon checked itself, then shook its body like a hellhound slipping its master's leash and leaped forward again. It was only a dozen steps away. Merrin smelled warm bile and felt cold breath. Still, he didn't retreat.

"By this sign of the Holy Cross, of our Lord Jesus Christ, who lives and reigns with the Father and the Holy Spirit—!" Merrin flung up his hand, like a traffic cop ordering a speeding truck to stop. A handprint slapped across the creature's gray cheek. It howled as loud as a freight train, but it didn't halt. Merrin yanked Francis's little crucifix from the chain around his neck and held it out before him. It seemed a futile gesture, like taking up a slingshot to fight a giant. Merrin's heart pounded, but he stood firm.

The creature galloped ahead, eight steps away. Five.

"God the Holy Spirit commands you!" Merrin boomed over the crucifix. *Sarah*, he thought, *fight it!*

The creature staggered as if struck. It screamed in obvious pain. Merrin's heart leaped. Joseph whimpered once behind him. The creature gathered itself on its impossibly twisted legs to rush forward one last time.

Merrin brandished the crucifix again. "The mystery of the Cross commands you!"

The demon recoiled a step as if it had been struck in the chest. Its tongue dripped algae saliva, and the green light of its eyes flickered. Then it bellowed and rushed forward, fast as a truck, unstoppable as an avalanche. Joseph screamed.

Fight it, Sarah! Merrin thought, and tightened his fist around the crucifix. "The blood of the martyrs commands you!"

The demon's head snapped back with an audible cracking sound, but its speed didn't diminish. Fear filled Merrin's chest and he could barely breathe, but he stood firm. "In God's name, demon, I CAST YOU OUT!"

The demon slammed into him. Merrin heard a horrible crunch, as if a side of beef had fallen five stories and hit a concrete sidewalk. It took Merrin a moment to realize that the sound hadn't come from him.

The creature's arms and legs snapped backward. Blood spattered the cave walls and floor as it bounced off the newly-formed fortress of Merrin's faith and crashed to the ground. Merrin stood in place, feeling solid and unmoved as stone. The creature groaned once, then fell silent.

The quiet, the absolute stillness, was unnerving. After a moment, Merrin picked out the sound of his own heartbeat and the rasp of Joseph's frightened breathing. The creature lay on its side with its back to Merrin. Merrin couldn't move. Blood oozed through the thin cloth of Sarah's dress. Still Merrin couldn't move. It was as if a firm, hard hand were pressing down on him, holding him still. Merrin looked at the creature's bleeding back, its shattered legs.

A small hand plucked at Merrin's shirt. "Father?" Joseph said.

The immobilizing pressure vanished. With a low cry, Merrin stumbled forward and dropped to his knees beside the ruined figure on the ground.

"Sarah?" he said. The skin on her arms and legs was no longer gray. "Sarah!"

A tiny, mewing sound. Merrin carefully rolled her over. Bones ground sickeningly beneath his hands. A lump closed Merrin's throat and tears stung his eyes.

Sarah looked up at him, her face clear of the demon. Bruises mottled her cheeks, and blood spilled freely from a cut lip. She stared up at him, eyes filled with pain.

"Lankester." The word was a mere whisper.

"I'm here, Sarah," he whispered back. "I'm here."

"You . . . saved me." A faint green light flickered in Sarah's eyes. It grew stronger and began to blaze.

Merrin grabbed her, pulled her tight against him. Anger battled sorrow inside him. *No. I won't let this happen to you. You're free, Sarah. You will be free!* Sarah shuddered hard, then relaxed in his arms. Merrin felt a rush of movement, a faint breath of air that sighed once and faded with a faint wail. Merrin looked down at the woman in his arms.

"Sarah," he said.

Her eyes closed, then opened. The green light was gone. "Lankester," she said in a weak whisper. "Help me."

Merrin's hands were wet. Warm blood was leaking from the back of Sarah's head. The leak spread. Scarlet life puddled, then pooled beneath her on the cavern floor, flowing from her broken limbs and crushed organs. Merrin looked down at her, desperate and powerless. He wanted to heal her, staunch the flow, but he didn't have enough hands. A moment ago he had been powerful as a mountain, but even a mountain couldn't heal the wounded.

"I'm sorry," he said softly. "I'm so sorry."

Sarah reached up to touch his face, then dropped her hand. "Thank . . . you," she said, "for freeing . . . me." Her eyes slid shut and her breath rattled in her chest.

Merrin swallowed hard, then carefully lay her down. He was only vaguely aware of Joseph padding over to stand beside him. The boy knelt, tears streaming down his face. He took Sarah's limp hand in his own.

"*Misereatur tui omnipotens Deus, et dimissis peccatis tuis,*" Merrin murmured, "*perducat te ad vitam aeternam.*" May almighty God have mercy on you, forgive you your sins, and bring you to life everlasting.

Fighting tears of his own, he reached down and made the sign of the cross on her forehead. When he finished, Sarah exhaled one more time and was still. Silent tears fell from Merrin's eyes.

"Father?" Joseph said.

Merrin rose and wiped his face on his sleeve. "She's with God now." He paused to let the words sink in—for himself as well as for Joseph. "She's with God."

It was Joseph who found an easier way out— another tunnel that exuded a sweet, fresh breeze. Merrin led Joseph toward increasing brightness, grateful he wouldn't have to crawl back through the claustrophobic tube. They emerged at the base of a rocky hillside into painfully bright sunlight. The dig site was only a few yards away, but Merrin saw no sign of the church. The sandstorm had buried it completely. An occasional bloody hand or broken leg poked out of the sand, as the only hints that a fierce battle had been fought here.

Crows croaked overhead, circling lower and lower. One of them landed on the sand next to a half-buried face, and Merrin recognized Emekwi. He led Joseph away before the boy could see. Once they were a safe distance away, Merrin paused long enough to hold out his hand and murmur last rites for the second time that day. He wanted to do more, but it was the best he could manage.

Epilogue

✠

Nairobi, British East Africa

Every burning conflict eventually settles into charcoal.

—Kenyan proverb

THE OUTDOOR CAFÉ smelled of tomatoes, coffee, and fresh-baked bread. Passers-by crowded the sidewalk, but automobile traffic was light. It was early winter, and there was a definite nip in the air despite the noonday sun. Merrin drew his coat more closely around him and sat down across from Semelier. The older man had traded white linen for brown tweed, though he still rested both hands atop his walking stick. A cup of coffee steamed on the table in front of him.

"It's freezing out here," Merrin said, blowing on his hands. "Why didn't you pick a table inside?"

"You've been in Africa too long, my friend," Semelier

241

laughed. "It's a fine day for coffee on the terrace." To prove his point, he took a long, slow sip from the cup. "Ah! Italian coffee is one thing I do miss when I have to be at home."

"And just where *is* your home?"

"That's not important," Semelier said with another sip.

A waiter bustled over, but Merrin waved the man away. Then he reached into his coat pocket and dropped a thick brown envelope on the table. Semelier raised his eyebrows in an unspoken question.

"It's your money back," Merrin said. "I didn't find what you were looking for."

Semelier smiled and shook his head. "But you found *something*, didn't you?"

"Did you keep that puppet?" Merrin countered. "You must be pretty good at it by now. Pulling strings, I mean."

"My good man, I have no idea—"

"So what are you?" Merrin interrupted. "Bishop? Cardinal? Abbot?"

"Fisher," Semelier said with an airy smile.

"Don't give me that bunk," Merrin returned. "Someone at the Vatican wanted me at that site, and you were sent to persuade me. You knew I wouldn't go if a representative of the Church asked me directly, so you pretended to be a black market dealer of antiquities. Francis said the Church knew the history of the site, and Nairobi has a cardinal, for heaven's sake. Any number of powerful people could have gone. Why go through the trouble of tricking *me*?"

"Ask them." Semelier gestured at the distant domes of the Holy See.

"I'm asking *you*."

Semelier sighed. "After all you have been through, Merrin, do you still think that evil is the only force in the universe that acts through men? Only one person could do what needed to be done at Derati. You yourself decided that the events in Hellendoorn may have happened in part to bring you there."

"How did you know that?" Merrin whispered, thunderstruck.

"You are angry because you believe the Church manipulated you," Semelier said, taking another sip of coffee. "So let me ask you something else: Why did you stay in Derati?"

The question caught Merrin off guard. "Stay? I . . . I had no choice."

"Oh? What power made you stay? You could have walked away any time you chose. Any number of other men would have. Why didn't *you*?"

"I couldn't leave Joseph in the hands of that creature," Merrin said simply.

"Let me ask you another question. If you could turn back the clock, would you still go to Derati?"

"Yes," Merrin replied without hesitation. Then a chagrined smile flickered across his face. "Yes, I would. My choice. But I still want to know who you—"

Semelier leaned across the table and pressed a finger to Merrin's mouth. It brushed his lips, light as a feather, but it halted his speech. "Don't worry about Joseph. He will be fine with Father Gionetti in

Nairobi. In the meantime, I am sure you can find a mission or poorhouse somewhere that could use the contents of that envelope. Good day to you . . . Father Merrin."

Before Merrin could react, Semelier rose from the table and disappeared into the crowd of passers-by. After a long time, Merrin left the café and headed up the street in the opposite direction. As he walked, his coat fell open, revealing a new black-and-white Roman collar.

Father Lankester Merrin paused to raise his head to the Roman sun. Then he smiled and walked with firm steps toward the domes and spires of the Vatican.

Visit
❖ **Pocket Books** ❖
online at

www.SimonSays.com

Keep up on the latest new
releases from your favorite
authors, as well as author
appearances, news, chats,
special offers and more.

SIMON & SCHUSTER
A VIACOM COMPANY
www.SimonSays.com

Pocket
Books

2381-01